Dead Man's Confession

Holmes

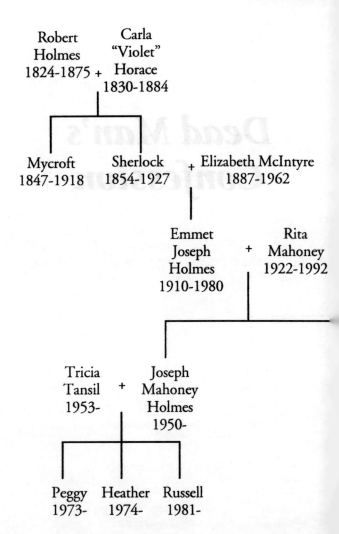

Robert Holmes 1824-1875 + Carla "Violet" Horace 1830-1884

Mycroft 1847-1918

Sherlock 1854-1927 + Elizabeth McIntyre 1887-1962

Emmet Joseph Holmes 1910-1980 + Rita Mahoney 1922-1992

Tricia Tansil 1953- + Joseph Mahoney Holmes 1950-

Peggy 1973-   Heather 1974-   Russell 1981-

Family Tree

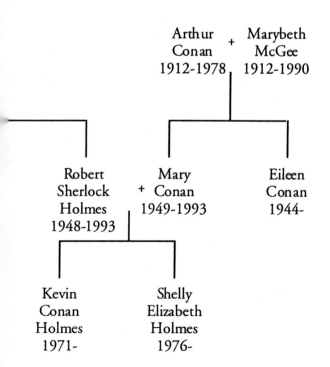

Arthur
Conan + Marybeth
1912-1978 McGee
1912-1990

Robert
Sherlock
Holmes + Mary Eileen
1948-1993 Conan Conan
1949-1993 1944-

Kevin Shelly
Conan Elizabeth
Holmes Holmes
1971- 1976-

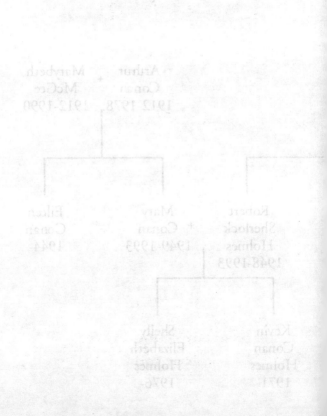

Adventures of Shelly Holmes™
Case #1

Dead Man's Confession

Cass Lewis

FamilyVision Press
New York

FamilyVision Press™
For The Family That Reads Together™
An imprint of Multi Media Communicators, Inc.

575 Madison Avenue, Suite 1006
New York, NY 10022

Shelly Holmes Adventures™, FamilyVision Press™
and For the Family That Reads Togetther™ are trade-
marks of Multi Media Communicators, Inc.

Library of Congress Catalog Card Number: 93-071557

ISBN 1-56969-150-9

10 9 8 7 6 5 4 3 2 1
First Edition

Printed in the United States of America

To RMC and RHF
for believing in me.

Chapter One

It was a beautiful day to be on a bike, thought seventeen-year-old Shelly Holmes as she pedaled down a quiet residential street in her hometown of Boston. The sun was shining strong after weeks of overcast weather and cool temperatures, as if announcing the dreary gray days of winter were now far behind. Shelly took this as a good omen as she pitted her strong, willowy legs against a short hill. Her high school days, like the gray skies of winter, were almost a thing of the past. She had only one more paper to write, and then it would be a downhill ride to graduation next week.

That last paper was an essay on Greek mythology for Mr. Kinnard's humanities class. It seems she wasn't the only one writing a paper on Greek mythology either. All the good books on the subject were checked out of the library.

So Shelly was on her way to Baker Street Books, a wonderful little shop packed to the rafters with books, books, and more books. The owner and proprietor, Nicholas Cramer, a family friend, had invited her to look around for anything that might help her with her essay.

Shelly reached the top of the hill and saw that Peppercorn Park had exploded in green in response to the recent good weather. The trees were covered with newly spread leaves, and the grass was thick and lustrous. Much as she wanted to get this last paper out of the way, Shelly couldn't resist a ride through the park. She was an avid photography buff, always on the lookout for an interesting shot, and she had her camera in her knapsack with her school supplies.

She coasted cautiously along the asphalt path that curved through flanks of green hedges. The greenery was already so thick in the park someone could be out of sight just ahead, and she didn't want to have an accident.

Shelly got off her bike and put up the kickstand when she was not too far from the little pond at the center of the park. Sometimes ducks gathered on the banks of the pond, and she wanted to see if she could sneak up on them and snap some photos.

A passing cloud suddenly cut off the sunlight as Shelly pulled the camera from her knapsack. She frowned at the sky. There hadn't been any clouds a minute ago, but there it was, a huge blob of gray that hardly seemed to be moving. Shelly decided that as long as she was here, she wasn't going to let the cloud ruin the opportunity for her. She adjusted the shutter speed and f-stop to compensate for the reduced sunlight and then crept down the path toward the pond.

As she reached the end of the hedge-lined

path, Shelly raised the camera and looked at the world through the viewfinder. She eased around the hedge into sight of the pond, and what she saw made her freeze in surprise.

There were no ducks on the near bank, only two guys a little older than Shelly, wearing black jackets and tearing the purse away from an elderly black woman who was huddled, sobbing, on the ground between them. Almost as a reflex, Shelly started hitting the shutter button on the camera. The black jackets were covered with pointy metal studs that formed the image of a dragon on the back of each. One of the guys wrenched the purse away from the old lady.

"We told you not to give us no trouble," the other one said.

Apparently they weren't just going to take the purse and leave the poor woman alone, Shelly realized. She pulled back behind the hedge and tried frantically to think of a way to help the woman. But what could she do? There was no time to run for the police. She was tall and athletic, but she knew she couldn't possibly deal with the two of them physically. She didn't have to fight them, she told herself, she just had to make them leave. But there was no way a blonde, teenaged girl in biking gear could scare off two tough gang-bangers...or was there?

Shelly dug her keys out of the pouch she wore at her waist and found the police whistle she carried on her key ring, a birthday gift she carried for several years. She filled her lungs and blew a sharp, loud blast that split the air in the quiet park. Quickly taking another deep breath, she shouted, "Freeze! Police!" in the most commanding voice she could manage.

When she peeked around the hedge again, she saw the two guys in black jackets sprinting in the other direction, the elderly woman abandoned on the ground behind them.

Shelly ran over to the woman. She seemed to be all right, though she was still crying. She looked up at Shelly and said, "They took my pocketbook. They pushed me down."

Shelly knelt down to her. "It's all right. They're gone now. Are you hurt?"

"No, I don't think so. I didn't have any money. I told them that, but they didn't believe me. They took my pocketbook anyway."

"It's okay," Shelly said soothingly. "My name's Shelly. What's yours?"

"Thelma. Thelma Rice."

"Do you think you can walk, Mrs. Rice? We need to go call the police."

Shelly helped the old woman to her feet and then along the asphalt path to a bench. Thelma was able to move fine on her own, so Shelly collected her camera and bike and walked her back to the entrance of the park. Shelly called the police from a pay phone there and then waited with Mrs. Rice on the bench for the patrol car to arrive.

She had stopped crying but now seemed dazed and numbed by the whole experience. Shelly tried to get her talking about something more pleasant and asked about her family.

"Oh my," the old woman sighed, some of the life returning to her face. "She'll be so worried. My daughter. That's where I was going, over to my daughter's place. I'm supposed to be baby-sitting my grandkids while she goes to work."

"It's okay," Shelly said. "Give me her phone number, and I'll call her for you."

The voice that answered the phone was full of dread—the daughter seemed to have sensed that something had happened. But Shelly quickly reassured her that her mother was safe and explained about the attack and that they were waiting for the police. The woman seemed very grateful to Shelly and asked her to tell Thelma not to worry, that she would get a neighbor to baby-sit the kids and that she would check on her at home tonight after she got off work.

Shelly relayed the message to Mrs. Rice and then kept her occupied talking about her daughter and grandchildren until the police arrived. By the time the cruiser pulled up and the two uniformed officers stepped out, she had recovered almost completely from her ordeal. Now, instead of shock and fear, she showed only a fiery anger at what had happened to her.

Shelly stood up and waved the police officers over to the bench where she and the victim had been sitting. As the officers came near, Shelly recognized the mustached Hispanic man on the left.

"Sergeant Garcia!" she exclaimed.

"Shelly!" he said, equally surprised to see her. "What are you doing here? We received a report that an elderly woman had been attacked in the park."

"I made the report," Shelly said. "This is Mrs. Rice. She was the one—"

"I was the one those two awful boys knocked down and robbed," Thelma said. "They took my pocketbook, and I want it back!"

Sergeant Garcia looked to his partner. "Lynn, you want to take Mrs. Rice's statement?" He turned back to Shelly and guided her a short distance away. "Now, why don't you tell me what you saw?"

Shelly told him about coming upon the two hoods and Mrs. Rice in the park and how she had scared them off. Sergeant Garcia grinned.

"Pretty clever," he said approvingly. "You're definitely your father's daughter."

At that moment, his partner came over to them with an open notebook.

"What have you got?" Garcia asked.

"Two guys, around twenty, dark hair, gang

jackets. Sounds like a couple of the Steel Dragons, but you know how many of them match that description?"

Garcia's partner glanced over at Mrs. Rice, and Shelly could read the frustration on her face, that the two attackers would probably get away with their crime. Shelly suddenly remembered something she had not yet told Sergeant Garcia.

"Oh yeah," she said, "before I scared the two guys off, I took their pictures." She gestured at her camera.

The surprise on Garcia's face lasted only a second, and then he started laughing. "You really are your father's daughter. Can I have the film?"

"Of course." Shelly began to rewind the film so she could remove it from her camera. Garcia's partner began to scowl again.

"How are we going to get it developed?" she asked Garcia. "With the cutbacks, we take it to the lab this time on a Friday afternoon, we're not going to get it back until late Monday at the earliest. Maybe we should look for a Fotomat or something."

"I know how to develop film," Shelly said shyly. "I could even make enlargements for you, if you've got a darkroom I can use."

Lynn gave her a look of amused wonder. "Who is this kid?"

Sergeant Garcia said, "Oh, I suppose I should introduce you two. Lynn Lauder, this is Shelly

Holmes, R. Sherlock Holmes's daughter."

That seemed to tell Lauder everything she needed to know. Shelly's father, a highly respected private investigator with an office here in Boston, often served as a consultant to the local police department. Lynn shook Shelly's hand and nodded. "That explains it, and then some. What do you think, Garcia? We get that film developed this afternoon, we've got a good chance of getting those two perps off the street tonight."

Garcia nodded. "I think we can find you a darkroom, Shelly."

On the way to the police station, they dropped off Mrs. Rice at her building. Before she went inside, she turned back to the cruiser and said to Shelly, "Thank you again, dear. Most people would have turned the other way instead of helping me. Nice to know there are still some good people in this world. Take care, dear."

"You too, Mrs. Rice," Shelly said, waving as the cruiser pulled away from the curb.

At the police station, Shelly saw a few more familiar faces, friends and associates of her father, but she didn't have time to say hi to them all. Garcia found her a darkroom to work in and then went down the hall to take care of some paperwork. The lay-out was different from the darkroom her mother had at home, but once Shelly found where all of the chemicals and supplies were stored, she had no trouble developing the film. She made several prints of the shots that most clearly showed the two attackers' faces, and then she went to find Sergeant Garcia.

He and Lynn were talking to a long-haired man in jeans and a T-shirt who was perched on Garcia's desk and sipping coffee from a styrofoam cup.

"Shelly," Garcia called when he saw her in the doorway. "Come in." He gestured to the man sitting on his desk. "This is Detective Brown, from the Gang Activities Section. He's familiar with the Steel Dragons and knows a good many of their members by sight. He may be able to recognize the two who attacked Mrs. Rice."

Shelly said hi to the detective and handed over the sheaf of photos she was carrying. He didn't look at them for more than a few seconds, and he was already nodding his head.

"Nice work," he said. "P. J. and Dodge. It figures. Those two just can't stay out of trouble." He looked up at Shelly. "But with these photos, nothing's going to keep them out of jail. Good job, young lady. A terrific piece of work. Are you planning on following in your father's footsteps?"

Shelly had been apprenticing at her father's office and was seriously considering it, but her

interest in photography made a career as a pho-
tojournalist also very tempting. She wasn't starting college until next fall, so she figured she had
time to make up her mind. However, this little
episode, the rush of knowing that she took the
photos that would be the critical evidence in
convicting two criminals, was swaying her
towards becoming a private investigator.

"I'm thinking about it," she said.

"Speaking of your father," Garcia said, "I tried
to call him to let him know where you were, but
he was out. I did talk to your mom, and she
made me promise to get you home in time for
dinner. Come on. Your bike's still in the trunk
of the cruiser. I'll give you a ride."

Shelly looked at her watch and was startled to
see how late it had gotten. Good thing that
humanities paper isn't due tomorrow, she
thought, but she would take this kind of action
over Greek mythology any day.

Chapter Two

When Shelly got home, she found her mother cutting up tomatoes for a salad.

"Hi, Mom, I'm home," she said, dropping her biking gear and knapsack on the kitchen counter. "What's for dinner?"

Her mother laughed as she mixed the tomato chunks into the salad. "Just like your father. Spend your day out fighting crime, and then you come home and want to know what's for dinner."

"Fighting crime makes you hungry," Shelly said.

Mary Holmes wiped her hands with a dish towel and tossed it at her daughter, who dodged and laughed. Mother and daughter had the same ocean-blue eyes and thick blonde hair, though Mary wore hers styled short rather than long and free like her daughter's.

"You better be hungry," her mother told her. "We're having spaghetti, and you're going to have to eat your father's share."

"He's going to be late?" Shelly asked, unable to keep the disappointment out of her voice. On the trip back from the police station, all she had been able to think about was telling him how she had helped identify Mrs. Rice's attackers.

Her mother read her face like a billboard. "Your father already knows all about this afternoon's adventure, and he said to tell you he's very proud." Her smile faltered a bit. "He also said you should get a good night's sleep. He's taking you on a stakeout tomorrow."

"Yes!" Shelly jumped up and did a little victory dance, pumping her fist in the air. She stopped when she noticed the distracted look on her mother's face. Her mother wasn't the only person who could guess someone else's thoughts. "You don't need to worry, Mom. I'm sure if he's taking me that there's going to be no danger."

"No," she said, "I wasn't worried about that…not exactly, anyway. It's just that you say you haven't made up your mind about your career yet…"

"I haven't," Shelly said.

"…but at times like these I see the same sort of intensity in your face that your father gets when he's following a hot lead. I guess I've gotten used to worrying about him being a detective, but when I think of you out there—it's a whole new kind of worrying."

Shelly hugged her mother and said, "There's no need to start practicing yet. Even if I do decide to become a detective, it's not like it's going to happen overnight. There'll be plenty of time to worry after I get out of college."

Her mother nodded. "You're right, of course. But that doesn't mean I'm going to stop worrying. Sometimes I just wish you'd let your artistic abilities develop more."

"I am," Shelly said. "With my camera."

Her mother's eyes narrowed slightly. "You do have a good eye, Shelly, but the way you use your camera—it's like your great-grandfather and his famous magnifying glass. A tool to help find the truth."

Shelly laughed. "I never thought of that. But I don't just take pictures of muggers and crime scenes, Mom. I went into the park looking for ducks. I have a serious interest in photography as an art form."

Her mother nodded. "I know you do. But now I think it's time to eat."

Shelly stepped over to the oven and sniffed the air. "Is that garlic bread I smell?"

Her mother laughed. "Don't eat too much or tomorrow might be your last stakeout with your dad!"

Shelly was so excited that she woke up before her alarm went off the next morning. After almost two years of working afternoons and weekends and summer days with Dad at the agency doing mundane tasks like filing and making phone calls, she was finally getting to go out in the field. Shelly opened the drawer of her nightstand and removed her diary and the English fountain pen her Aunt Eileen, her mother's sister who lived in London, had sent her for Christmas last year.

Shelly updated her diary with yesterday's events and reflected on what her first stake-out would be like:

> I think letting me go on this stakeout
> is Dad's way of telling me he's proud
> of me for keeping my head yesterday
> and helping to nail those two mug-
> gers. Sometimes I wish he would
> come right out and say things like
> "great job" and "I'm very proud of
> you, Shelly," instead of making me
> read between the lines, but then he
> wouldn't be Dad, I suppose.

When she finished recording the whole adventure, Shelly put her diary away and hopped out of bed to get ready. As she padded down the hallway to the bathroom, she listened for any sounds indicating whether her father was up yet but she didn't hear any. She showered, brushed her teeth, got dressed, and then headed down-stairs.

Shelly wondered how she would deal with leaving this house to go to college next fall. She and her brother Kevin, who was an actor in New York, had grown up here. She had never lived anywhere but in this old Tudor house at the end of their dead-end street. Over the twenty-five years they had lived here, her parents had added on to it several times, constructing a library/study after her father's agency took off and a sculpture studio and darkroom for her mother, an accomplished and respected artist. It would be strange leaving this house, but at least she had a few more months before she had to deal with it.

Shelly made herself some wheat toast in the kitchen and then went to her father's study to see if he was up yet. Sure enough, light was pouring from the partially open door. Her father's piercing gray eyes looked up from his desk at the sound of Shelly's light knocking. The look of intense concentration he wore softened when he saw her, and he smiled. It was a smile that would have startled his co-workers and colleagues, who knew R. Sherlock Holmes as a serious and determined man who overlooked no detail and was relentless in his pursuit of the truth. But it was a smile Shelly knew well, one she liked to think he saved just for her.

"Morning, Dad," she said as she squeezed through the partially open door into the cluttered study. The room, like his office downtown, was modeled after that of his famous grandfather, Sherlock Holmes of 221B Baker Street, London, England. But while the office downtown was polished and ordered, with gleaming oak paneling and books lining the shelves neatly and evenly, the study at home seemed the very height of disorder. Files, books, and newspapers were stacked seemingly at random around the room, and the desktop was a clutter of folders and photographs. At the office, R. Sherlock had his wonderful secretary, Mrs. Dunn, to maintain order, and for that he was grateful, since he liked to make a good impression on his clients and other visitors. However, here at home he indulged his natural penchant for what seemed to be chaos.

In actuality, he knew what was in each stack and could put his hands on any article or dossier he needed in only a few seconds. Shelly understood this aspect of his character entirely; she had a tendency to do the same thing, though her mother was not as indulgent when it came to her daughter's bedroom.

"Good morning, sweetheart," R. Sherlock greeted his daughter, shuffling the papers and photos in front of him back into a file folder. "Are you all set for your first stakeout?"

"I think so," Shelly said. "I just need to get my camera. How much film should I bring?"

R. Sherlock pondered the question. "Let me see, 36 exposures per roll...I think three rolls should be more than adequate." He had a deep, commanding voice that resonated throughout the room, though he spoke in quiet tones. He wouldn't have even needed the whistle to scare off those two muggers yesterday, Shelly thought. A few sharp words with that voice, and they would have been gone. "I see you've had breakfast," he said, glancing at the bit of wheat toast folded in Shelly's hand. "Make sure you go to the bathroom—"

"*Dad!* I'm supposed to be your assistant today, not your daughter."

He gave her the smile again and nodded. "Very well, assistant. I'll meet you at the car when you're ready."

Shelly backed out of the room and popped the last bit of toast into her mouth. She jogged upstairs and collected her camera, then went outside, where she found her father standing next to his Dodge Aries, admiring the rose garden in the early morning sunshine.

Even dressed informally in a polo shirt and canvas slacks he looked distinguished. At 45 years, he was turning gray at the temples, but combined with his high-bridged nose and intent gray eyes it only made him seem more imposing, much like his famous grandfather, for whom he was named. His full name was Robert Sherlock Holmes, but his mother had always called him "our Sherlock," which had evolved into his nickname, R. Sherlock, by which everyone knew him. Even his business cards listed him as

R. Sherlock Holmes, and he looked every bit as impressive as the name suggested.

The car, however, left something to be desired.

"Dad, why don't you get a new car?" Shelly asked. "Something with some real horsepower and a little pizzazz. And maybe a CD player."

Her dad shook his head and opened the passenger-side door for her. "The customized engine in this car has more horsepower than a Corvette. As for pizzazz, pizzazz is the last thing a private investigator wants."

"Thomas Magnum drove a Ferrari," she said as she got in. "A Ferrari's got mondo pizzazz."

Her father opened the driver's door and climbed in. "Thomas Magnum was on TV. He was looking for ratings. We're looking to be inconspicuous. We need a car that no one is going to notice even if it's parked across the street from their house around the clock for a week."

"In that case," Shelly said, "I think you made the right choice. But I still prefer Mom's Lincoln."

Her father started the car and winked at her. "Truth be told, I prefer Magnum's Ferrari myself."

Forty minutes later the car was snugly parked between two others across the street from the

Omnidial Corporation's office in Waltham, a western suburb of Boston. R. Sherlock had parked at the rear of the three-story building, so they had a view of a vacant parking area, a dumpster, and the gold-glass facade of the building itself.

"Okay, so are you going to tell me why we're here?" Shelly asked. Not knowing was killing her.

R. Sherlock said, "Yes, but have your camera ready. Omnidial hired me because somehow someone has been stealing their proprietary telephone access codes. With these codes, crooks make thousands of dollars of long-distance phone calls without paying for them."

"If we're looking for somebody, what makes you so sure they'll come out the back?" Shelly asked.

"Not so fast," her father said. "I've been over every bit of information supplied to me by the company, and I've been over all of their employment records. You have to have a magnetic keycard to get into the place, and their computer security is top-notch."

"So it must be an inside job," Shelly said.

Her father gave her an enigmatic smile. "That's what the vice president in charge of operations thinks as well."

"And you don't?" Shelly asked.

"I have a theory," was all R. Sherlock would

say. "We're here this morning to see if it's cor-
rect."

"Okay," Shelly said. "So what exactly are we
looking for?"

R. Sherlock frowned. "Your great-grandfather
would have said that if you look for just what
you want to see, you're likely to miss everything
else. He made the simple skill of observation
into his most valuable tool as an investigator. So
let us observe, and we'll draw our conclusions
from what we see."

This answer didn't satisfy Shelly, but she knew
it was all she was going to get from him for now.
Anyway, talk of her great-grandfather always
stirred her interest, and while she had her father
trapped, she decided to try to worm a story or
two out of him.

"Do you remember my great-grandfather?"
she asked.

"No, he died many years before I was born.
But my father knew him as well as anyone could,
and he told us—your Uncle Joe and me—all
sorts of stories. Your Grandpa Emmet had quite
a way with words and a remarkable memory.
His father had stressed that he develop his skills
of observation, and they served him well, both as
a storyteller and as a New York police detective."

A distant look and a hint of a frown came
over R. Sherlock's face as he spoke. Shelly could
guess what he was thinking about. His father,

Grandpa Emmet, had wanted him to become a New York City policeman like himself. He hadn't understood R. Sherlock's need for independence, his need to work on cases of his own choosing and in his own way. R. Sherlock and Grandpa Emmet had argued so vehemently about it that they didn't speak to one another for months afterward. They patched things up before Grandpa Emmet passed away, but Shelly knew her father still harbored regrets that his father couldn't understand or support his decision. She decided she should distract him before he really started brooding.

"So which one of the stories was your favorite?" she asked.

The question seemed to take him by surprise, and then he had to put some serious thought into his answer, which was just the distraction Shelly had been trying to provide. When he looked up reflectively to reply, all traces of brooding had gone.

"That's a difficult question to answer," he said. "Each of Sherlock Holmes's adventures was unique and enthralling, and your Grandpa Emmet had a knack for telling each one just right. But if I was forced to choose one, I suppose my favorite is one that's about the man himself and not some baffling mystery."

Shelly didn't think she'd ever heard this one before. "Tell me," she said.

Her father seemed to be distracted as a back door opened in the Omnidial building and two men in gray uniforms came out with a cart filled with plastic garbage bags. They pushed the cart to the dumpster and began heaving the bags into it. R. Sherlock glanced at his watch.

"Is this something?" Shelly asked. "Should I be taking pictures?"

"No, not yet," he said. Then, as if nothing had interrupted them, he returned to the subject of his grandfather. "My favorite Sherlock Holmes story takes place after the great fight between him and his nemesis, Professor Moriarty, the 'Napoleon of Crime.' Both were assumed to be dead after they plunged off a ledge high above the Reichenbach Falls in Switzerland. Sherlock, however, survived the fall and fought the raging waters to reach the shore. The experience left him bruised and battered and badly shaken up, so much so that rather than announce his miraculous survival to the world, he allowed his friends to believe he was dead....even Dr. John Watson, his closest friend and the man who had chronicled many of his adventures.

"Holmes needed time to recover, physically and spiritually. The bruises and abrasions were gone within days, but the psychic trauma of coming so close to death was slower to heal. To help speed his recovery, he did what many people do in times of emotional need: He went home. Home in this case was the bleak northern reaches of England. He stayed in a small farmhouse on the Yorkshire moors and apparently found solace in the bleak landscape, for Grandpa Emmet always said he spoke of it with affection."

Shelly knew he would have denied it, but she thought her father was as good a storyteller as Grandpa Emmet. She would have told him so, but she didn't want to interrupt.

"One gray morning while Holmes was playing his violin, serenading the desolate countryside, a sweet voice began to sing along. He turned to find a young local girl walking with a basket of bread, and according to Grandpa Emmet he fell in love on the spot. The girl's name was Elizabeth, and she was just 21 years old. In those days, most women were married with several children by that age, but Elizabeth was an independent type. She had had offers of marriage, but she had felt that her true love was somewhere in the world, and she was prepared to wait all of her life to meet him if it proved necessary. It didn't. She met him that day."

"That's really romantic," Shelly said.

Her father nodded. "Though he was 20 years her senior, they married a short time later and had one son, Emmet Joseph Holmes. Eventually Sherlock had to return to London, as his services were needed and, once he had recovered from his near death at Reichenbach Falls, he had become restless to be once again on the trail of a mystery. He told no one of Elizabeth and young Emmet, so that they would be in no danger from his many enemies, but he made secret journeys to Yorkshire to visit his wife and son from time to time until he finally decided to retire. Then they moved to New York City, where they happily lived out their final days."

After he finished, Shelly said quietly, "I can see why that one's your favorite. I think it's mine, now, too."

"You're named after them, you know, Shelly Elizabeth. You've got his mind, and her beauty and independence."

"I wish I had a picture of the two of them together."

Her father looked thoughtful. "Back at the office I have a box of old letters and notebooks that I inherited when Grandpa Emmet died. I believe there are some photographs in there as well."

"Really? You've had them that long and never gone through them?"

Her father seemed as surprised by this as she was. "Yes, well, some of your grandfather's papers are in there as well. It seemed too painful to go through them at the time, so I put the whole box in the safe to go through later. I suppose I've been finding reasons to put it off ever since."

"Enough of that," Shelly said firmly. "We should do it soon, maybe even today if we get done at a decent hour."

"And we might at that," R. Sherlock said with an edge creeping into his voice.

Shelly looked across the street to see what had captured her father's attention. At first all she noticed was that an old Volkswagen van had parked in the rear lot. Then she realized some-one had gotten out of it, a man with greasy, dark hair and glasses. As she watched, he walked over to the dumpster and climbed inside.

Chapter Three

Shelly stared hard at the dumpster, wondering if she had really just seen a man climb into it.

"Get his picture when he comes out," her father murmured.

Shelly raised her camera and focused on the dumpster. She wondered why on earth anyone would do such a thing, but she trusted her father to know what he was doing. After thirty seconds or so, the man's head poked out and looked around. Shelly's blood went sub-zero when his glance passed over her, but he didn't seem to see them in the Dodge, and a moment later he climbed out of the dumpster. He was a young white male, about five-ten, heavyset, with dark, greasy hair and wearing thick, dark-rimmed glasses.

Shelly snapped picture after picture of the man hoisting himself out of the dumpster, dropping to the asphalt, and then pulling out two plastic trash bags, which he hauled swiftly to his Volkswagen van. He tossed them inside and then ran to the driver's door.

"Is the license number clear?" her father asked.

"No problem," Shelly said. "I can blow it up as big as your desktop if you want."

"Large enough to read clearly will be sufficient," he said dryly.

The van backed out of its parking space and headed out of the parking lot. R. Sherlock started his car's engine and eased out onto the street. He drove to the next corner just in time to see the van pulling out into traffic in front of them.

"Very neatly done," Shelly said. "Did you plan it that way?"

Her father smiled but said nothing.

"So what's he doing with two bags of trash?" Shelly asked. "Is someone on the inside hiding the access codes in the trash?"

"No," her father said. "Not a bad idea, but I don't think so."

Shelly was dying to know what was going on and had a hundred other questions to ask, but the car got onto busy Route 128 and was traveling well above the speed limit. Her father had to concentrate to keep up without being conspicuous about it, and Shelly didn't want to distract him.

The van exited Route 128 ten minutes later, and R. Sherlock followed it to a residential area. The van pulled into a driveway next to a small redbrick house. R. Sherlock lingered at the corner long enough for Shelly to snap shots of the dark-haired man carrying the trash bags into the house. Then he pulled away.

Shelly could tell by the look on his face that

he was pleased. "Can you tell me what's going on now?" she said.

"I'll tell you what I know," he said, "and you tell me what you think."

"Okay," Shelly said, resisting an urge to say, 'finally.'

"As part of the regular activities at Omnidial, they generate several kinds of reports, a couple of which list the various access codes that the company uses, along with how often they've been used and so on. That vice president I told you about assured me that the illegal users were not getting the access codes from these documents because, as part of the security measures he himself implemented, the company purchased a document shredder. The two reports with access codes on them are shredded." He looked over at Shelly. "And only those reports."

The significance of this dawned on Shelly, and she suddenly realized why they'd spent their Saturday morning as they had. "So if you were to go into Omnidial's trash and find the shredded pieces, you'd know they were all part of the reports with the codes listed on them. They'd be a pain to reassemble again…"

"But if you stood to make a few hundred thousand dollars," her father finished for her, "the effort would be worth it."

"So you found out when they put their trash out and watched to see who came and got it,"

Shelly said.

Her father nodded. "It's a little more complex than that. They get several pick-ups each week, but the report in question is generated on Wednesday and usually shredded on Friday. The cleaning crew puts out the trash Saturday morning, but it's not picked up until Monday morning. We got lucky that our bad guy is impatient."

"So what next?" she asked.

"What's next is that you develop those pictures for me and then I go to the police. We'll get a warrant to search that house on the basis of the evidence we've collected so far, and I'm sure we'll find further evidence on the premises to incriminate everyone involved. So how soon can I expect prints and negatives on my desk?"

"After we get home, an hour, tops." Shelly marveled that once again a case depended on her developing photographs to serve as the critical evidence. She was in heaven.

The next day was Sunday, and Shelly got to sleep in. When she finally got up, she padded down the stairs and found her mother sitting at the kitchen table with a plate of banana-nut muffins and the Sunday paper spread out in front of her.

Shelly kissed her good morning and asked, "Where's Dad?"

"He got a phone call earlier and said he had to go out." Mary passed her daughter the comics section and a muffin.

"Did the search warrant come through?" Shelly asked with some excitement. She wished she'd been able to go along on the raid, but she knew her father would never have allowed it.

Her mother gave her a sour look. "I don't know," she said. "He didn't say." Then her face brightened. "I have an idea. You helped your father in his line of work yesterday. How about helping me in mine today? I've got some dark-room work that needs to be done for my latest sculpture."

"Sure," Shelly said brightly. Then a look of doubt crossed her face.

"What is it?" Mary Holmes asked. "Do you already have plans?"

"No, it's not that," Shelly said. "It's just that I've still got to work on my humanities paper, or I'm not going to graduate Friday. I did most of the work yesterday afternoon, but I've still got a few pages to go."

"I won't keep you more than an hour or so," Mary said.

"Okay," Shelly said, splitting open her muffin and reaching for the butter knife. "It won't take me long to finish anyway."

The phone on the hall table rang. Mary looked up from the section of the paper she was holding, but Shelly had already set down her muffin and was standing. "I'll get it," she said.

Shelly jogged into the hallway and answered the phone. "Hello."

"Hi, Shelly," said the familiar voice of her older brother.

"Kevin! How's New York?" Her brother, 24 years old, was an actor. He had started in commercials when he was three, then had become the smart-mouthed little brother on a sitcom, and now was a 'leading man on daytime television'—a hunk on a soap opera. He did have the looks for it, Shelly had to admit. He was tall, blond, and classically handsome, and every one of her friends was in love with him.

"Hot, humid, and noisy," her brother answered, "but I love it. How have you been?"

That was all the invitation Shelly needed. She pulled the phone cord around so she could sit on stairway and then launched into the stories of Friday's adventure with Mrs. Rice and Saturday's with her father.

"Wow," he said when she finished. "It sounds like you've had one heck of an exciting weekend."

"But not as exciting as next weekend," she said. "I can't wait to graduate. And I can't wait to see you."

Kevin cleared his throat. "Uh, that's sort of why I called, Shell. I'm sorry but I'm not going to be able to make it back to see you graduate."

Shelly tried to keep the disappointment out of her voice. "How come?"

"I was offered a really choice part in *A Midsummer Night's Dream,* which is being produced as part of the Shakespeare in the Park series. The guy playing Oberon backed out, and they picked me to replace him, but they've already started rehearsals and I've already missed so much that I can't possibly miss any more."

Shelly didn't say anything. After a few seconds, Kevin continued. "This is a real shot for my career, Shell. Having one of these productions on your resume scores a lot of points in the respectability department. Look, I'll get you tickets for opening night, and you can come up and see me in my stage debut."

"Yeah, I wouldn't miss it for anything," she said, trying not to sound spiteful. It was exactly what he had said about coming to her graduation.

"Thanks for understanding, Shell. And good job on the detective work. It's real obvious who inherited Sherlock's genes in this generation. Hey, I'll talk to you soon. And say hi to Mom and Dad for me."

"Okay. Bye." Shelly hung up the phone but continued to stare at it.

Her brother. She loved him dearly, but that only made these little disappointments more painful. He was too good-looking for his own good, she thought. Most people saw him as a sort of golden boy, but they didn't know him like she did. He could be the most self-absorbed, self-serving, manipulative person she knew without even being aware of it.

Like when he decided to hire an agent. Up until that time, Mary Holmes had served as his agent, manager, and chauffeur. Without even consulting her, Kevin went out and got what he called a "real" agent and announced it to the family without even considering that she might be upset after all of the time and energy she had put into his career. Later, he announced he was changing his stage name to Kevin Conan, adopting his mother's surname, he said, to recognize all of her effort on his behalf. What a crock, Shelly thought. His agent had probably suggested he change his name to get rid of his child-actor image, and Kevin had probably thought "Kevin Conan" sounded cool.

So, though she was disappointed, she wasn't really surprised he wouldn't be coming to see her graduate. It's probably for the best anyway, she thought. Kevin was used to being the center of attention and had a way of stealing the spotlight on any occasion. Friday was going to be *her* day.

Shelly looked up when Mary entered the hallway.

"Who was on the phone?" her mother asked.

"Kevin. He's going to be too busy to come to my graduation Friday."

"What do you mean 'too busy?' That boy can be so thoughtless. Don't worry, dear, I'll call him and tell him…"

"No, don't do that," Shelly said. "It's okay. He just got a good part in a play and it sounded important. Anyway, I was thinking of asking Mr. and Mrs. Dunn if they want to come. Is that all right with you?"

"Of course," Mary said. She was wearing that proud parent smile that always embarrassed Shelly. "I think they'll be honored to come."

Shelly stood up and returned her mother's smile. "Good. Now just let me finish my breakfast and then let's hit the darkroom."

Chapter Four

Monday morning started with Shelly's father knocking on her door and shouting, "Shelly, are you up? It's getting late."

Shelly squinted drowsily at the glowing red numbers on her clock, but when she saw that classes would be starting in less than half an hour, all traces of sleepiness vanished. "Oh my gosh." She threw back the covers and bounced out of bed. "I'm up, Dad!" she called. She had been up late working on her paper and must have forgotten to set her alarm. She'd never make it to school on time riding her bike.

"I'll drop you off at school on my way to work," her father called through the door as if he had read her mind. "I'll be downstairs when you're ready."

"Thanks, Dad. I'll be down in a flash."

She wondered why her mother had not gotten her up before this, and then remembered that she was casting her latest sculpture today. She was always out of the house by 5:30 A.M. on days when she was casting, which left Shelly and her father on their own to get ready for school and work. It figured that'd be the day she'd forget to set her alarm.

Shelly got ready in record time and then shot

down the stairs with her knapsack hanging from one shoulder. She grabbed a couple of granola bars from the kitchen, and then found her father waiting for her in the car. She hopped in next to him and collapsed onto the seat. There's nothing like oversleeping to get your adrenaline going in the morning, she thought.

Her father seemed amused. "You only have to make it through a few more days, sweetheart, then it'll all be over."

"Easy for you to say." She ripped open one of the granola bars and offered him the other, but he shook his head. "I did finally get my paper finished last night, though. Do you think if I drop by the office this afternoon Mrs. Dunn will have time to type it for me?"

"You'll have to ask Mrs. Dunn," her father answered. "We'll be doing the paperwork to wrap up the Omnidial case today."

"Okay." Mrs. Dunn was more than a secretary to R. Sherlock. She took care of all the mundane details of running the agency, leaving him free to devote his particular gifts to the cases he handled. Shelly liked her a lot, and the feeling was mutual. Mrs. Dunn's typing of Shelly's papers had less to do with R. Sherlock being her boss than with Mrs. Dunn and Shelly being friends. Shelly was looking forward to inviting her to Friday's graduation ceremony, and she'd be able to do that this afternoon too.

Besides, she thought, how much paperwork could there be left on the Omnidial case? When he had come home last night, her father had told her all about the raid. The police had captured all three men involved in stealing Omnidial's access codes and had found the reassembled reports and other evidence to make an airtight case against them.

As they reached the entrance to the school, another thought occurred to Shelly. "Dad, do you think that when I come by this afternoon you might have time to look through that box of papers and photos of Grandpa Emmet's with me?"

Her father thought about it for a moment and then nodded slowly. "I believe I will." He smiled. "It's a date. Have a good day at school, sweetheart."

"See you then. And thanks for the ride."

The morning classes dragged for Shelly, but the afternoon was given over to graduation rehearsal, which wasn't so bad. Shelly's class marched back and forth through the auditorium while the band played "Pomp and Circumstance" a few times, and then they mostly goofed off while Joanne Chung practiced his valedictory speech. They had to remain in their seats and Shelly wasn't near any of her friends, so she slipped on her headphones, concealed by her long hair, and scanned the radio dial for cool tunes. Then, after a squirt-gun fight broke out in the back rows, Vice Principal Thorne decided to let them go early.

When she reached her locker, Shelly found Amanda Blaine and Kay Delaney waiting for her. They were two of her best friends. Kay, a pretty girl with freckles and the school's number-one track star, had been friends with Shelly since kindergarten. Amanda was a tall, brunette who had moved to Boston from Georgia several years ago and was one of the brightest and funniest people she knew.

"I swear, if I had to listen to Joanne's speech one more time today I'd spontaneously combust," Amanda said as Shelly reached them.

"At least you two got to sit near each other," Shelly said as she spun the dial on her locker.

Kay slipped a finger under Shelly's hair and hooked the headphones she was still wearing. "Yeah, you poor thing. While we were listening to Joanne's speech for the tenth time, you were jamming to U2."

"INXS," Shelly corrected, laughing with them. As she pulled her knapsack from her locker and slammed the door, the three girls were joined by the fourth member of their unofficial little club, Maria Rodriguez, this year's head cheerleader. All of them were a little boy-crazy, but Maria was the craziest, they all agreed.

"Hi, Maria," Kay said. "Did you see Toby Ryan today?"

Shelly could feel herself blushing. They all knew she had a crush on Toby, and they liked to tease her about it.

"As a matter of fact, I did," Maria said, smiling mischievously.

"And," Kay said with an identical smile, "did he happen to ask about our friend Shelly here?"

"Cut it out, Kay," Shelly said. "I don't care who Toby asks about. Let's talk about something else."

The other three laughed. Kay put her arm around Shelly's shoulders. "Look, Shelly, we're just thinking about you. The school year is almost over. If something's going to happen between the two of you, it has to happen soon."

The other two nodded solemnly. Shelly shrugged out from under Kay's arm and glared at her.

"Why don't you worry about your own love life?" Shelly said a bit louder than she had intended. "I don't see the boys knocking your door down. I'm out of here."

"Whoa, hey," Kay said, her smile gone. "I didn't mean anything, Shelly. Look, I was just poking a little fun. I'm sorry."

Shelly looked at her sharply, as if she were going to snap at her again, and then she started laughing. The others, relieved, laughed with her.

"No, I'm the one who should be sorry, Kay. You didn't go over the line. We ride each other harder than that all of the time. I guess I'm just a little sensitive at the moment. What you said about time running out for me and Toby—I've kind of been thinking the same thing."

"Well," Kay said brightly, "what do you say the four of us go split a pizza and discuss tactics. You've still got a few days left, plus graduation."

"And my open house afterwards," Maria piped in.

"I'd really love to," Shelly said, "but I've got to go down to my Dad's office."

"Yeah, and I have to get home," Maria said. "I promised my mom I'd baby-sit my little sister."

Amanda nodded. "I've got to work at four."

Kay threw up her arms. "Fine. Go your separate ways. But Shelly, I'll call you tonight."

"So will I," Maria said.

"Me too," Amanda chimed in. "Maybe we should set up a conference call."

"Between us, we'll think of something," Maria said as the four of them headed down the hallway toward the front of the school. "Toby's too cute to let him get away."

"Speaking of cute," Amanda said, poking Shelly, "is your brother going to come for graduation?"

Shelly sighed. "No. He's in some big play he

has to rehearse for."

"Bummer," Amanda said.

At the front entrance, the four of them said their good-byes. Shelly paused to dig her bus pass out of her purse, and Maria noticed her pull it out.

"Do you want a ride, Shelly?" she asked. "I practically go right past your father's office on my way home."

"Sure, thanks," Shelly said. She didn't much like riding the bus. She sort of wished she had her own car, like Maria did, but she had discussed it with her parents. Though they wanted to buy her a car, they were thinking ahead to her college career. Shelly was planning on going to the University of Colorado. Considering the cost of out-of-state tuition as well as travel expenses, her parents couldn't afford to send her to college *and* get her a car. Shelly had understood and was not too upset. She could ride her bike to most places, and her parents were very flexible about lending her their cars. Still, at times Shelly did long to have a car of her very own. Riding in Maria's Mustang was always one of those times.

Maria dropped Shelly off in front of her father's office building. "I'll call you tonight," Maria called as she drove off. Shelly waved as the car pulled away from the curb and shot down the street. She considered herself very lucky to have such good friends as Maria, Amanda, and Kay. She would miss them a lot when she went away to college.

Shelly rode the elevator up to her father's floor and then walked down the hallway to the glass doors with R. SHERLOCK HOLMES, PRIVATE INVESTIGATOR stencilled on them. Shelly pulled the doors open and entered.

The outer office had been decorated as a Victorian sitting room. A small chandelier shone elegantly over an oblong table that displayed recent magazines. High-backed chairs and a long sofa were arranged around a stone fireplace where, in the winter, electric logs provided a cozy glow. In one corner opposite the entrance a grandfather clock marked time with somber chimes on the quarter hour. In the other corner, beneath an oil painting of Sherlock Holmes and Dr. Watson pursuing a wolfish silhouette across the English moors, was an immaculate antique desk bearing an array of modern equipment—computer and printer, telephone, answering machine, fax machine. Next to it were two filing cabinets and a photocopier.

This desk, Mrs. Dunn's, was the nerve center of the office's administration, but Mrs. Dunn was not in evidence. Shelly leaned over the desk to look at the telephone display and saw one of the lines was busy. She heard the squeak of her father's double office doors behind her and turned to find Mrs. Dunn emerging.

"Hi!" she said.

"Hello, Shelly," Mrs. Dunn greeted her. She was 58 years old and had been Mr. Holmes's secretary since Shelly was a little girl. Today she was wearing a burgundy dress with a ruffled front. Her reading glass hung from a chain around her neck. Shelly noticed from the spring in her ginger-colored hair that she'd gotten a new perm recently.

"I like your hair," Shelly said as Mrs. Dunn took her seat behind her desk.

Mrs. Dunn put hand up to it and smiled. "Why, thank you, Shelly. My husband didn't even notice, but you and your father both mentioned it. You can't slip anything past a Holmes."

"It's in the blood," Shelly agreed.

"So, Shelly," Mrs. Dunn asked. "Is this purely a social visit, or is there something I can do for you?"

Her father had mentioned the paper to Mrs. Dunn, Shelly could tell. "Actually, I have a couple of reasons for being here. First, do you have time to type a paper for me? The very last one of my high school career."

Mrs. Dunn chuckled. "Of course, Shelly."

"Second, Kevin isn't going to be able to make it to my graduation, so I was wondering if you and Mr. Dunn would like to join us. It's at 5:30

Friday afternoon."

"Yes, I know," Mrs. Dunn said, pointing to the day on her desk calendar, which was circled several times in red and written over with SHELLY'S GRADUATION!!! in large red letters. "We would be honored to attend. Mr. Dunn and I play bridge Friday nights, but we can make our bridge date a little later this Friday. I'll check with him and let you know for sure."

"Great," Shelly said. She rested her knapsack on Mrs. Dunn's desk and pulled out the sheaf of handwritten pages that was her Humanities paper. She handed it to Mrs. Dunn. "It's on Greek mythology."

Mrs. Dunn slipped her reading glasses on. "That will make a nice change from telephone access codes."

"Thanks, Mrs. Dunn. Too bad you won't be in Colorado to type my papers in college."

Mrs. Dunn tapped the fax machine on her desk with her fingernails. "You can always fax them to me."

Shelly laughed. "Dad would love that," she said, but she stored that possibility away in her mind for future reference.

The light on the telephone went out, indicating R. Sherlock was no longer occupied. Mrs. Dunn said, "Your father's free now, Shelly. You can go on in."

"Thanks again, Mrs. Dunn," Shelly said as

she stepped to the double doors. They opened with their usual, drawn-out squeak, like the door to a mausoleum or haunted house. One time, the maintenance man was in the office to replace burned-out light bulbs, and while he was at it he oiled the doors to R. Sherlock's office to get rid of the squeak. When R. Sherlock found out, he thanked the maintenance man and then explained that he *liked* the doors to squeak, so no one could enter his office without alerting him to their presence. The maintenance man, who was something of a fan of R. Sherlock's, replaced the hinges on the doors with unoiled ones that squeaked like the lid of Dracula's coffin.

The other security measures in the office were a little more high-tech. The chandelier concealed a closed circuit television camera connected to a monitor on her father's desk, so he could keep tabs on who was in the outer office, and a top-of-the-line alarm system protected the place during the off-hours. Sometimes Shelly thought her father indulged in this cloak-and-dagger stuff a little too much, but she had to admit she had a weakness for it too. Her favorite of the agency's secrets was in her father's office.

R. Sherlock's business office was much like his study at home, lined with bookshelves and furnished in the same Victorian fashion. But it did have several major differences. The most striking was that this office was much neater, as neat as a museum, and had several framed documents on the wall, his degrees, his license, several commendations from the police department, and one from the governor. Authentic items from his grandfather's office were displayed in a glass case, most notably Sherlock Holmes's pistol and pipe and his famous magnifying glass. Behind the desk, flanking a large window granting a view of the city were two portraits, one of Sherlock Holmes, the other of his son, R. Sherlock's father, Emmet Holmes, in his old-fashioned police dress uniform. On one side of the room, over a sofa, hung a portrait of Holmes's sinister nemesis, Dr. Moriarty. On the other side were several dark oak file cabinets, which Shelly knew very well from her hours as R. Sherlock's file clerk. On top of them were several of Mary Holmes's bronze sculptures.

Shelly's favorite secret of the office was concealed in a low oak cabinet pushed out of the way against the wall next to the door. It looked light, as if she could easily push it around the room if she wanted, but in actuality it was anchored into the floor. The polished marble top of the cabinet slid smoothly to the side, revealing a heavy steel door with a combination lock. Inside this safe was where R. Sherlock kept his most important papers, and this was where she found him when she entered the office.

He had the cabinet top moved to the side and the safe door wide open and was rooting through the papers and envelopes inside. His hands emerged holding a plain cardboard box whose only distinguishing features were a colorful cluster of canceled stamps and an address label. It was not very large, perhaps one foot square and six inches deep, and the packing tape that had held it closed had been sliced open.

"Hi, Shelly," her father said, grinning as he held up the box. "Ready to travel back in time?"

Chapter Five

R. Sherlock locked the safe and concealed it once again. Though they would only have the box out a little while and then would be returning it to the safe, Shelly knew it would have run against R. Sherlock's rigid security procedures to leave the safe open even for so short a time. He carried the box to the sofa, and Shelly followed him.

"Is the Omnidial case all wrapped up?" Shelly asked as she curled her legs up under her on the sofa. "I don't want to keep you from your work." The cardboard box with its colorful assortment of stamps separated her and her father.

"It's finished," R. Sherlock said, sounding pleased. "I made my report to the vice president of operations today, and they'll be instituting new security measures to keep the same thing from happening again. From now on, they won't just be shredding the most important documents; they'll be shredding *all* documents. *Nobody* will be able to reassemble any critical documents again."

"I wouldn't have thought anyone would be able to reassemble one shredded document," Shelly said. "That was really pretty clever."

"The man responsible, James Hunt, does seem to be a brilliant individual," her father admitted. "When the police raided his house, in addition to the Omnidial material, they found evidence that he had gained access to many other systems, including the city's 911 emergency system. He could have caused a great deal of chaos. The city is going to have to revamp the system's security."

"How much time do you think he'll do?" Shelly asked.

"A few years, probably, at a minimum security institution."

Shelly shook her head. "I don't understand why he didn't just get a real job. With his talents he should be able to make major bucks legitimately."

Her father shrugged. "Criminals of that sort are often in it for the intellectual challenge and the thrill of defeating a formidable security system as much as for the money."

"I guess someone like that would have no problem breaking in here," Shelly said, looking around the room that she had been thinking was so secure a few minutes ago.

"Breaking into this office would require a completely different set of skills, Shelly. Not only does the building have 24-hour security, but this office has its own independent alarm system. Besides, as long as I've been here there's never been a break-in attempt."

"That you know of," Shelly pointed out.

"Yes," her father conceded with a smile. "As far as I know there's never been a break-in attempt. Now, are you ready to take a look in this box, or do you want to grill me some more?"

Shelly laughed. "Sorry, Dad. Let's open the box now."

They pulled back the cardboard flaps together and revealed a layer of overlapping black-and-white photographs. They pulled them out one by one and examined them. R. Sherlock was able to identify most of the people and places in them.

The first was so old it had become brittle and begun to crack around the edges. It was not so much in black-and-white as in faded shades of brown. But despite the effects of age on the photo, its subject still maintained a haunting beauty. A young woman in an elaborate long-sleeved dress and matching hat, she seemed to look right into Shelly's eyes as she handled the photo delicately by the edges. The eyes of the woman in the photo had a depth and clarity that drew Shelly to them. Though it was impossible to tell their color in the photo, Shelly was sure they were blue.

"That's your great-grandmother Elizabeth McIntyre Holmes, taken right after she and Sherlock were married. Grandpa Emmet told me that when Sherlock returned to London after recovering from the incident at Reichenbach Falls, he took this photograph with him. The marriage had to be kept secret at that time, and though he did sneak away to visit her in Yorkshire when he could manage the time, they were apart more often than not. He used to keep this photo hidden under his desk blotter, where he could pull it out from time to time and just stare and think of her."

"This very picture," Shelly said breathlessly, awed by the sheer romantic significance of a single photograph. She found herself wishing she could take a picture that would hold such meaning for someone.

Shelly gently set the photo aside and pulled another from the box. This one showed a young boy in a cowboy outfit perched on the back of a pony. "That's your Grandpa Emmet," R. Sherlock said, "when he was, oh, about five years old."

The next photo was another very old one. A thin young man in an English school uniform stared out from the photo with a piercing and unmistakable intensity.

"Sherlock Holmes," her father said.

"He looks about my age in this one," she said. She tried to imagine what the great detective would have been like at her age. Somehow, she didn't think he was worried about finding the right dress for graduation and making an impression on Toby Ryan.

They continued to sift through the old photos for the next hour and a half, and some of them inspired her father to tell stories about the people they depicted. Her father was even in some of them, a bright-eyed boy between a young-looking Grandpa Emmet and Grandma Rita. There was even a picture from *his* high school graduation. He seemed tall and thin, even in his cap and gown, and his solemn expression reminded her of the photo of Sherlock Holmes. There was a definite resemblance, she thought. Though he denied it, R. Sherlock seemed pleased that Shelly saw one.

When they had examined each and every photo, a bulky manila envelope several inches thick lay revealed in the cardboard box R. Sherlock pulled it out and undid the red thread wrapped around brown cardboard buttons that was holding it closed. Then he carefully shook it until its contents began to spill out onto the sofa between him and Shelly.

"It's full of envelopes," Shelly said, puzzled. They were of all sizes and colors and looked old. The ink of the addresses and the cancellation marks had faded gray, and the stamps themselves were not ones Shelly recognized. She picked up a handful of letters and began looking through them. They were all addressed to Sherlock

Holmes in New York, and many were unopened.

"Excuse me, Mr. Holmes," Mrs. Dunn's voice suddenly called from the intercom on his desk. "Your wife is on line one."

R. Sherlock glanced at his pocket watch as he rose from the sofa and stepped to his desk. His eyebrows rose in surprise when he saw the time. He punched a button on the telephone and picked it up.

"Hi, dear," he said. Shelly observed the sudden brightness in his face and found herself hoping that she would find someone to love as much as her parents loved each other. Then she started thinking about Toby again, and Kay's comment about time running out for them.

"That sounds great," R. Sherlock was saying. "We'll meet you there in twenty minutes." A pause. "Certainly. All right, good-bye."

He hung up and turned to Shelly. "Your mother has come up with an idea I think you'll like," he said. "She suggested we meet her at the mall for dinner, and then afterwards we can shop for a graduation dress for you."

"'We?'" Shelly said, raising an eyebrow. The thought of her dad shopping for a dress made her smile. She could just picture him walking stiffly through the aisles of Bloomingdale's, hands clasped behind his back, examining the selection with his penetrating gray eyes and a look of solemn concentration on his face. Shelly had to put a hand to her mouth to keep from giggling.

"Well, you and your mother can go dress shopping," R. Sherlock said uncomfortably. "I'll pass the time in the book store."

"Sounds good, Dad," Shelly said, the laughter still in her voice. She would have to remember to paint that particular mental picture for her mother while they were shopping. She would appreciate it as much as her daughter, Shelly was sure.

She looked down at the letters spread out before her. "All of these are addressed to Sherlock Holmes," she said.

Her father nodded. "After he retired to New York, he tried to maintain a low profile, but people still found out where he was and wrote to him to solicit his help with various puzzles and problems. Not being the type of man to retire completely, and always unable to resist a good mystery, he consulted by mail on a number of cases. After he passed away, letters continued to arrive, and Grandpa Emmet saved them." R. Sherlock looked at his watch. "I'm sure there are some fascinating stories in there, but they'll have to wait for another afternoon. Your mother will kill us if she has to wait."

"Okay," Shelly said, helping her father pack everything back into the box. As they replaced the layer of photos on top of the manila envelope, she said, "You know, Dad, it's really a shame to keep these photos shut up in the safe."

Her father nodded as he closed the box. "I was thinking much the same thing. Perhaps that can be a project for you when you start coming in days next week. We'll get a photo album, and you can mount them in some kind of sensible order with typed descriptions."

"That sounds great!" Shelly said. She had been working in the office in the afternoons and on weekends since her sophomore year, and full-time during the last two summers. She had been looking forward to coming back full-time this summer, but now even more so.

R. Sherlock took the box back to the oak cabinet and slid the marble top to the side to reveal the safe.

"Let's see," he muttered to himself. "My birthday's April 1st." He spun the dial around a couple of times, finally stopping on 1. "Your mother's birthday is March 16th." He turned the dial the other direction to 16. "Your brother's is January 29th, and yours is August 30th." He finished entering the combination, the dial set on 30, and he turned the handle that opened the safe.

"Dad, you're not supposed to use obvious numbers for a combination." Shelly was surprised that Mr. Security himself would do such an amateurish thing.

Her father glanced at her over his shoulder and winked. "Well, Shelly, the way I figured it," he said as he turned back to the safe and stowed the box inside once again, "if someone made it past the building security, my alarm system, and all of the other security precautions, then they could probably open any safe without any trouble. So why not make it easy on myself? Besides, a criminal of that caliber would assume I would not be so foolish as to use my family's birthdays for the combination. I'm covered either way."

Shelly laughed and shook her head, finding her father's logic a little too convoluted for her taste. "Come on, Dad. Let's go meet Mom before you give me a headache."

They opened the squeaking double doors and found Mrs. Dunn separating sheets of paper that had poured from the computer printer on her desk. "Good timing," she said to Shelly, handing her the pages. "Here you are: one humanities paper. Nine pages long, and it reads very well, Shelly. An A for sure."

"Thanks, Mrs. Dunn," she said. "You're a lifesaver."

"Are you ready to call it a day?" R. Sherlock asked his secretary.

"I believe so," she said, switching off her computer.

R. Sherlock set the alarm system, and then the three of them left the office. The glass doors locked automatically behind them with an authoritative click, and they headed for the elevator.

On the way down, Mrs. Dunn said, "Oh, Shelly, I talked to Mr. Dunn about attending your graduation ceremony. Sidney said he would be honored and delighted. He wanted very much to take you and your family out to dinner afterward, but regretfully he cannot because of our bridge date."

"That's very kind of Sidney," R. Sherlock said, "but we're planning a graduation dinner Saturday night, and we'd love it if you could both join us."

The elevator had reached the parking garage, and as the three of them exited the elevator into the underground garage, Mrs. Dunn said, "That would be perfect for us."

"Terrific," Shelly exclaimed, her voice echoing from the concrete walls. They reached Mrs. Dunn's Toyota, and she waved as she unlocked the door. "Good night, Mrs. Dunn," Shelly called. "Thanks again for the typing."

Shelly and her father continued on until they reached his Dodge. After they got in, R. Sherlock reminded her, "Lock your door, Shelly. It's the first thing you should do when you get in a car...especially in our line of business."

"'*Our* line of business'...that sure sounds

good, doesn't it, Dad?"

R. Sherlock smiled and gave her a one-armed hug before starting the car. "It sure does."

As it worked out, after a laughter-filled dinner at Legal's restaurant, her father's beeper had gone off and he had driven home, leaving Shelly and Mary to shop for a dress. When the two of them arrived home, after 9:00 P.M., Shelly found her father in the kitchen.

"Any luck?" R. Sherlock asked when she walked in and dropped her purse on the kitchen table.

"No!" Shelly said, aware she had almost shouted the word and not caring after the frustration of the last couple of hours. "Shopping with Mom is a drag. Everything is too short or too tight or too 'far out.' I don't even know what 'far out' means!"

R. Sherlock was trying not to smile. "It couldn't have been that bad, Shelly."

"Oh yeah? Mom is determined to see me in a Laura Ashley dress. I mean, I thought great-grandmother Elizabeth looked absolutely beautiful in that photograph we looked at this afternoon, but I don't want to dress like her!"

Mary Holmes entered the kitchen behind her daughter, smiling wearily. "I don't think your father would have approved of either of the outfits you had your heart set on, Shelly. A red leather jumpsuit just doesn't seem right for a high school graduation. And that purple dress..." Mary drew an imaginary hemline across her upper thigh with her hand "...was just too short."

"I was just going to fix myself a bowl of mint chocolate chip ice cream," R. Sherlock said lightly. "Anybody interested?"

Shelly knew he was trying to break the tension, but her frustration wouldn't dissipate quite so easily. "No thanks," She said. "I promised Kay and Maria I'd call them tonight. I'd better do it before it gets too late."

As Shelly left the kitchen, her father was laying out two bowls, spoons, and the carton of ice cream on the table for him and his wife.

Upstairs, Shelly closed her door and got out her diary. She did intend to call her friends, but she would wait until she was changed and ready for bed, so she could talk with the lights out and just go to sleep when she was finished. Before that, though, she wanted to record today's events in her diary. Between going through the box at her father's office and going dress shopping with her mom, she had a lot to write, and she filled almost four pages.

Finally she put the diary away and got ready for bed. After she had changed into her nightshirt and gotten under the covers, she picked up the phone on her nightstand and dialed Maria's number. Maria had her own phone line, so Shelly wasn't worried about disturbing Maria's parents. Must be nice, Shelly thought. Though her father had a separate line in his study, too many times had he or her mom picked up the phone while she was having a private conversation. Her own phone was something else to look forward to this fall.

Maria answered on the second ring.

"Hi, it's Shelly. I didn't wake you, did I?"

"No," Maria said. "I was just reading."

"Yeah?" Shelly said. "What?"

"Nothing, just some trashy romance novel. And speaking of romance, what are we going to do about you and Toby Ryan?"

Shelly sighed. "I don't know."

"Well, then, you're lucky you have me to do your thinking for you. I've got an idea."

"Okay," Shelly said warily, not yet daring to hope. "Let's hear it."

"I invited Toby to the open house party that I'm having Friday night after graduation."

"You invited everyone," Shelly said.

"Yeah, right. Anyway, you're always afraid to talk to him because you don't have anything to talk about. So talk to him about the party. All you have to do next time you see him is say hi and ask him if he's coming. If he isn't, tell him he's going to miss a good time. If he is, tell him you'll see him there. Who knows? Maybe he'll ask you to go with him. The worst thing that can happen is you find out he isn't coming, and then you'll have a chance to talk him into it."

Maria stopped talking, and for a few second's Shelly could hear the faint background buzz on the phone line.

"Well?" Maria said.

"I'm thinking," Shelly answered. "I'm thinking that that's a really good idea. As long as I don't get tongue-tied or lose my voice or throw up on his shoes."

"Jeez, Shelly, you don't make this easy. Look, we'll practice tomorrow before you see him. I know it seems scary, but just think about where it might lead."

And as she drifted off to sleep that night, that's exactly what Shelly was thinking about.

Chapter Six

Tuesday morning went much more smoothly than the previous one. Shelly's alarm sounded at 6:15 A.M., and she got ready for school at a leisurely pace that was a far cry from yesterday's mad rush. She lingered over choosing what to wear, looking for something 'far out' to blow her mother's mind, but she finally settled on a pair of Levi's and a T-shirt her brother Kevin had brought her from Hawaii, with a surfing shark wearing sunglasses on the front and the name of a surfboard rental outfit on the back.

When she went downstairs for breakfast, she found only her mother in the kitchen. Shelly thought she looked sort of lonely, puttering around the kitchen all by herself, and Shelly wondered how her mother would cope after she left for college. After Kevin had left home, Mary Holmes had been sad for a while, but she'd still had Shelly, and their relationship had grown even closer. Shelly's departure would leave a much larger hole in her mother's life. And one in mine, Shelly thought.

"Morning, Mom," she said as she headed for the refrigerator. "Where's Dad?"

Her mom was pouring coffee into a mug Shelly had bought her years ago that said "Old

Sculptors Never Die—They Just Chip Away" on the side. "He got called downtown early this morning by the police."

"The police?" This sparked Shelly's interest. "Is he consulting on a case with them?"

"I'm not sure what's going on," Mary said tiredly. She took a long sip of coffee. Shelly got the idea that she had been awake for a while.

Shelly was fixing herself a bowl of Fruit Loops across the table from her mother when her mother noticed what she was wearing and laughed. "Is that the shirt your brother gave you?" she asked.

"Uh huh," Shelly confirmed. "Not too 'far out' for you, is it?" The cheer faded from her mother's smile, and Shelly realized she may have said it a little too pointedly.

"Look, Shelly," she said. "I'm sorry we couldn't reach an agreement about a dress last night. Maybe my senses of decorum and fashion are a couple of decades behind, but this is a very special occasion."

Shelly was nodding. "I know, Mom. I suppose I'm not the easiest person in the world to shop with."

"No," her mother said with gentle sarcasm. Her face took on a comically horrified expression and her hands went to her face like the kid in *Home Alone*. Doing an exaggerated impression of Shelly, she shrieked, "No, Mom! Are you out of your mind? That dress goes all the way down to my *knees!*"

Shelly laughed so hard she almost choked on her Fruit Loops. "I wasn't *that* bad, was I?" she asked when she could talk again.

Mary's eyes turned toward the ceiling. "Hm. Well, maybe not quite. Look, Shelly, I spoke to Aunt Tricia last night, and she told me about this great boutique on Newbury Street. If you're willing to give it another shot, I'll pick you up after school today and we can go try on a few."

"Okay," Shelly said, "but only if you promise not to use the words 'far out.'"

"Deal," her mother said.

School that Tuesday was not too bad, Shelly thought. If every day had been so much fun and so little work, high school would have been a lot more tolerable. She turned in her essay to Mr. Kinnard and felt as if a huge weight had been lifted from her. That was it! Nothing left to do but coast through graduation.

At lunch she got together with Maria, Kay, and Amanda. They didn't see Toby Ryan around, but Maria pretended to be him and Shelly practiced talking to him. It wasn't very serious, not with Kay and Amanda critiquing her performance with comments like "Suck in your stomach more" and "Run your fingers through your hair—guys like that." By the end of the lunch period they were giggling so hard they couldn't understand anything each other was saying. If Toby had seen her then, Shelly was sure he would have thought she was a lunatic.

But she didn't see Toby during lunch or for the rest of the day, though her friends were keeping their eyes peeled. They met briefly at the end of the day and determined to try harder tomorrow, as tomorrow was the last day of classes. Thursday they were off, and Friday was the graduation ceremony itself.

After they went their separate ways, Shelly went out front and found her mother waiting for her. They went downtown to Newbury Street, which was crowded with shops of all sorts. Shelly could have spent hours just looking in windows. They had no luck in the boutique her Aunt Tricia had recommended, but they stumbled across another place where they finally were able to find something mutually agreeable. It was black and sleeveless and fit Shelly perfectly. Mary thought it was a little too tight and a little too short, but she was able to live with it. Shelly was absolutely ecstatic. She almost said, "Toby will *die* when he sees me in this," but caught herself. Her mother didn't know a thing about Toby, and for now Shelly wanted to keep it that way.

After they bought the dress, they went out to dinner at a Chinese restaurant that caught their eye to celebrate. They got home pretty late, but Shelly's father had still not returned. Shelly really wanted to go running with Spike, but her parents didn't like her to go running at night.

Spike was a big klutz of a German shepherd owned by Julie Edwards, a friend of Shelly's. Julie taught at Harvard and didn't have a lot of time to walk Spike. Shelly loved to run with him, almost as much as Spike did, so Julie had given Shelly a key to her apartment and told her to come get Spike whenever she wanted to. Shelly and Spike ran together almost every day, but things had been so busy lately with graduation coming up and detective work and all that it had been almost a week since Shelly had seen Spike. She missed him. Tomorrow, she promised herself, she would take him to the park and let him romp in the grass.

When Shelly had finished writing in her diary and turned off the lights to go to sleep that night, her father still had not returned.

The next morning when she bounded down the stairs toward the kitchen, she was delighted to her the deep and commanding tones of her father's voice. When she entered the kitchen, she found him seated at the table with her mother. His suit seemed a bit rumpled, and there were shadowy crescents beneath his eyes. His tie hung loosely, and his collar button was undone.

He seemed tired, though he greeted her cheerful-
ly enough.

"Good morning, sweetheart," he called.

"Jeez, Dad, you look like you slept at the bus
station."

"Actually," he said, stretching, "I haven't slept
at all. I'm about to retire upstairs for a little nap
before I go back downtown."

"Wow," Shelly said, "this must be one rough
case you're working on."

"Two rough cases, actually," he muttered. It
was a slip he probably wouldn't have made if he
were well rested, but it *was* a slip, Shelly could
tell by the way her mother frowned and the way
her frown made R. Sherlock wince.

"Anything you need help with?" Shelly asked
without much hope of a positive answer. Over
the years, her mother had gradually come to
accept Shelly's interest in her father's career and
breakfast table discussion of his cases, but there
were two areas that were still taboo: messy
divorce cases and messy murder cases. Shelly
and her father had come to refer to such cases as
Unmentionable.

"No," her father said. "In fact, you don't need
to bother coming in any afternoons to work this
week. I'll be swamped, and I'm sure you'll be
busy with graduation plans. You will still get
paid, of course."

"Cool," Shelly said. "So these two Unmentionable cases you're working on—murder or divorce?"

R. Sherlock glanced at his wife. "One of each, and I think we've talked about them enough. Let's move on to something cheerier. Mrs. Dunn said she and Sidney will be able to join us for your graduation dinner on Saturday."

"Great," Shelly said. "Let's see, there's the three of us, the two of them, Julie, Gail, Aunt Tricia, Uncle Joe, and the cousins—twelve people all together. This is going to be fun."

She was looking forward to seeing all of them. Uncle Joe was her father's brother and also the detective agency's accountant. When they got together, the talk tended to turn toward business, but Aunt Tricia and Shelly's mom were used to it and usually let them alone and had their own separate conversation.

Shelly would spend the time catching up with her cousins, who were a precocious and talented group. Peggy, the oldest, was in medical school at Harvard, and Shelly had hardly seen her since she'd started classes there. Heather, who was only two years older than Shelly, was studying engineering at M.I.T. and working part-time as an auto mechanic. She knew more about cars than anyone Shelly knew, including all the guys at school with their rebuilt Camaros and T-birds. And last there was twelve-year-old Russell, who knew more about computers than his teachers at school but who tried to hide it so he wouldn't be branded a nerd, which he definitely wasn't. Shelly had told him so, but cousins had to say that sort of thing. He was also a film buff, and he and Shelly usually went to the movies together at least once a month.

"Shelly, are you going to need a car Friday night?" her mom asked. "I know you're going to Maria's open house, but are you driving or is someone taking you?"

Shelly sensed a deeper question, like did she have a date or was she going to hang out with her girlfriends? She felt like snapping back that it was none of her mother's business but restrained herself, in case the question was innocent. "I'd like to drive, if it's not a problem," Shelly said.

Her mother nodded. "I'm just asking because your father and I are going out to dinner with Uncle Joe and Aunt Tricia Friday night. It's no problem. We can go over to their house in your father's car and then go on to dinner in Joe's BMW."

Shelly's mom didn't like her father's car any more than Shelly did, and she realized without asking that Shelly wouldn't want to drive her friends around in the beat-up old Dodge.

"Thanks, Mom," Shelly said. "Well, I've got to get going to school. Looks like good bike weather."

"Looks like good sleeping weather to me," her father said as he stood up. "Have a good day, sweetheart."

"You too, Dad. Mom, I'm going running with Spike after school so I won't be home until 5:30 or so."

"Okay, Shelly. Enjoy your last day of high school."

Shelly turned out to be right: It was good bike weather. Morning sunshine washing over the world made every color brighter, but there was enough of a breeze to keep her cool and to make the hair that stuck out from beneath her biking helmet whip around behind her. If this hadn't been the last day of school, she would have been sour about having to spend the day inside, but since she would never have to go again, she didn't mind. Still, when she reached the school yard, it seemed the ride had lasted only a few minutes, and she was sorry it had to end.

She locked her bike in the rack in front, and when she looked up she say Kay, Amanda, and Maria waving at her as they came down the sidewalk. Kay was wearing a gorgeous satin jacket that looked new. It seemed too warm for a jacket, so Shelly figured Kay was wearing it to show it off.

"Hi, folks," she said to the trio as they reached her. "I love your jacket, Kay. Where'd you get it?"

"Graduation gift from my big sister," Kay said proudly, holding up her arms and twirling. The sunshine gleamed on the shiny material.

"The loot's already rolling in," Amanda said. She held out her arm and displayed an exquisite silver watch on her wrist.

Maria grabbed her forearm and took a close look. "Jackpot," was all she said.

"It's going to look great with the dress I'm going to wear Friday," Amanda said. That thought seemed to spark her memory. "How's the Great Dress Hunt going for you, Shelly?"

"Bagged one last night," Shelly said, as she unsnapped and removed her bicycle helmet. "You'll die when you see it."

"Yeah," Maria said, "but will Toby die when *he* sees it?"

Kay tapped Shelly's shoulder. She was looking down the sidewalk, the way they had come from a few minutes ago. "Speaking of Toby," she said, "here he comes."

Shelly looked up from stuffing the helmet in her knapsack, hoping Kay was playing one of her little jokes. Sure enough, here came Toby, shuffling along next to Mike Thompson and laughing about something.

"Great," Shelly whispered, "and I have helmet hair."

"Pretend like you're picking up something off

the ground and flip your hair back when you stand up," Amanda suggested.

Shelly tried it and then glanced around at her friends, who were smiling encouragingly. Amanda gave her a thumbs-up.

"Remember," Maria said, "ask him about the party."

Shelly looked to see how close Toby had gotten and felt light-headed. This is ridiculous, she thought in some small, detached part of her mind. She and Toby had been assigned as partners on a chemistry project back in March. She'd had no problem talking to him about Bunsen burners and pipettes. They'd even flirted with each other then and afterwards…at least Shelly had thought they were flirting. What if he didn't think so? No matter how logically she tried to think, his soft brown eyes slightly hidden by thick, curly, brown hair turned her mind to marshmallow. It wasn't a fluke that the senior class had voted him most handsome.

Mike saw them and elbowed Toby over closer to them. "Hi, girls," Mike said. "How's it going?"

Shelly missed Maria's reply. Toby had walked right up to her, and the rest of the world didn't register. "Hi, Toby," she said.

"Hi, Shelly." He wasn't really looking at her. At first Shelly thought he was looking for someone else, but then she started to get the idea that he was just as nervous as she was. "Are you going to Maria's open house Friday?" he asked.

She vaguely heard Kay and Amanda clowning around behind her but ignored them. "Yes, I am. I was hoping I'd see you there."

"You were?" Now he looked right at her, and there was a genuine happiness in his smile. "Well, I'll be there, and you'll definitely see me."

"I'll be watching," Shelly said.

"Good," Toby said. "Well, I guess I'll see you then. It's going to seem like a long time until Friday."

Shelly felt like she was going to explode in golden light so bright it'd make the sun seem dim. Instead, she nodded and said, "I know what you mean. See you then."

As Toby and Mike pulled away and headed for the building's front entrance, Shelly's friends closed around her. None of them said anything until the two boys had gone inside.

"Yes!" Shelly sang. She collected high-fives from each of them, and they congratulated her and complimented her on how cool she had been until the first bell rang and they all scattered to their homerooms.

Shelly spent the rest of the morning replaying the encounter in her mind and daydreaming about what Friday might bring. At lunch she and her friends planned the details of meeting at Maria's house after graduation and getting the place ready for the party. It was going to be quite a bash.

Afternoon classes were shortened so that they could attend one final graduation rehearsal. As the long double line of students marched through the auditorium, like zombies, Shelly thought with a smile, she spotted Toby in line next to Judy Raines. Toby saw her smile and returned one of his own. The rehearsal seemed to end soon after that.

Shelly stuffed everything that was left in her locker —which wasn't much after having turned in her textbooks on Monday—into her knapsack and hauled it out to her bike. Other seniors were laughing and shouting, hugging each other and honking their car horns as they burned rubber out of the parking lot. Shelly felt the same excitement, but she felt a little sad, too. There was a lot that she wouldn't miss about this place, but there were a few things she would: a few teachers, a few friends, and that's what made her sad. But there would be enough time for being sentimental later, she decided, and as she pedaled her way out of the parking lot, she screamed and hollered with the rest of them.

Chapter Seven

It was normally only a fifteen-minute ride to Julie's place from the high school, but Shelly dallied on the way, stopping to take pictures of freshly bloomed tulips and a group of kids playing on a jungle gym, so it took her closer to half an hour to reach her destination.

Of course, it wasn't *really* Julie's place, the upper floor of a grand old house that was practically a mansion. She lived there, but how that had come to happen was kind of complicated. Julie's mother, Ruth, was a sorority sister of Shelly's mother at the University of Chicago, as well as another woman named Joan Kennedy, whose family owned the house Julie lived in. When Julie decided to do her graduate work in sociology at Harvard, her mother, who was always doing this sort of thing for her, called her sorority sisters in Boston. Joan Kennedy, whose family spent most of the time at their home in the Virgin Islands, offered to rent the top floor of their Boston house to Julie. It had been converted into a separate apartment and seemed perfect.

Julie never liked her mother's interference, but this time she gave in, as the place was a dream apartment, with two large bedrooms, two and a half bathrooms, a den, an immense living room, a guest room, and a kitchen with a deck that overlooked the backyard.

It had been almost two years since Julie had driven up from her native Florida in her Range Rover. Julie's mother had arranged for her other sorority sister, Mary Holmes, to meet and greet her, and that's when Julie had met Shelly as well. Shelly was fascinated by Julie's area of expertise, deviant and criminal behavior, and she had absolutely fallen in love with Julie's six-month-old German shepherd, Spike, who had fallen in love with her in turn. That first night Shelly had volunteered to help take care of Spike, and that had been the beginning of a wonderful friendship. Though Julie frequently joked that Shelly liked the dog more than her, Shelly considered Julie one of her best friends.

Shelly bumped her bike up the curb into the Kennedys' driveway and followed it through the grounds and around to the side of the magnificent house. Julie lived in the apartment with a roommate, Gail, but neither's car was parked outside at the moment. Shelly made sure she had remembered her key as she climbed the heavy plank stairway on the side of the house, the independent entrance to the apartment. By the time Shelly reached the top, she had her key in hand and opened the door.

Spike was right there waiting for here. No

longer a lanky, clumsy six-month-old, Spike was now a hulking, clumsy beast who never failed to make Shelly laugh with his antics. She kneeled down in the doorway, and he greeted her in his customary manner, with lots of snuffling noises and sloppy kisses.

"All right, okay, that's enough, Spike!" she finally called out, laughing and giving him one last hug. She pushed herself to her feet and stepped aside to let him out the door. "Wait for me," she said as he dashed past and pounded down the stairway with enough noise to drown out a cattle stampede. "I'll be down in a minute."

She knew him well enough to know he wouldn't leave the grounds without her and didn't give it a thought as she made her way through the sunny apartment. There was only a counter area separating the living room from the kitchen, and the back wall of the kitchen was made entirely of glass, floor to ceiling. The living room itself had large picture windows and several skylights under which hung lush green plants in macramé holders.

"Julie!" Shelly called as she padded across the living room carpet. "Gail!" The place was quiet, but Shelly thought she should make sure there was no one home. Julie's roommate, Gail, a Jamaican with a musical voice and the most beautiful exotic eyes, was a graduate student in computer science and tended to spend hours in front of a glowing monitor, the only sound the occasional clicking of the keyboard as she typed in instructions. There was no answer to Shelly's call. They were probably both still at the university, she figured.

Shelly went into the guest room, which was almost like a second bedroom to her. She had spent a number of weekends here with Julie and Gail, watching videos, playing with Spike, and generally having a good time. Framed prints of Degas and Klimt hung on the bedroom walls, and gauzy curtains framed the windows. A queen-sized bed with a pastel bedspread dominated half of the room. A matching love seat and chair, and a desk were arranged in the other half, and a small color TV on the desk was aimed at the bed, where Shelly had been watching cartoons during her last visit. Her home away from home. Julie and Gail liked to joke with Shelly about when she was going to start paying rent.

She went to the closet and pulled out the gym bag she kept there to hold her running gear. After she changed into her Nike shorts, a tank top, and her joggers, she put her hair in a ponytail and was ready to go.

She found Spike waiting for her at the bottom of the stairs, looking up with that expectant happy-puppy face that always made her laugh, his tail whapping excitedly against the house's brick foundation.

"All right, all right, I'm coming," she called as she hurried down the steps. "Don't knock the place down."

She had brought Spike's leash, though she couldn't remember ever having needed it. Removing it from its hook in the pantry was a signal to Gail and Julie that she had taken him for a run.

Shelly jogged down the driveway toward the street, Spike trotting along without having to be called. He was something else she was going to miss when she went away to college. Running wouldn't be the same without him.

They followed Shelly's usual route, which took them through the affluent residential area where the Kennedys had their home, and then out and around the rolling emerald hills of the Dubliners Country Club Golf Course. The course was crowded today, with garishly clothed golfers swinging their clubs and caddies trailing after with their golf-bag burdens. Shelly didn't understand the appeal of the game, but she loved the course itself, so green and perfect without seeming artificial. Even the air seemed to be fresher and more invigorating.

After she had nearly circled the entire golf course, Shelly cut around the local elementary school and saw two Little League teams playing tee-ball in the diamond behind the building. Not long after that, they were back in Julie's neighborhood, and Shelly raced Spike the final few hundred yards to the driveway. He won, as he always did once he figured out she was trying to beat him.

Shelly walked up the driveway to cool off and saw that Gail's car was now parked near the bottom of the stairway leading to the apartment. Shelly wiped the sweat off her forehead with the back of her hand and laughed at Spike, who was practically running circles around her. She was exhausted, her leg muscles feeling like warm caramel stretched to the limit, and he was ready for another few miles.

"Nobody likes a show-off, pal," she said, lunging at him. He sprang playfully away and then rushed back at her. They kept up their mock battle, chasing and feinting at each other, until they reached the stairs. Shelly ran up, trying to block Spike from getting ahead of her, but there was no stopping him. He plowed past her and then sat at the top with his tongue hanging out, waiting for her to catch up.

"I'll get you tomorrow," she said as she opened the door. Spike squeezed in past her and lumbered toward the kitchen.

A surprised cry of "Hey, dog, watch yourself!" in a Jamaican accent told Shelly that Gail was in the kitchen.

Shelly followed Spike and found Gail fixing herself a salad. Her thick black hair was barely contained by a crimson-on-white jungle print scarf. She wore a matching blouse that looked terrific against her dark, coffee-colored skin and tan slacks and sandals. Spike was forcing himself underfoot, trying to get her attention. Gail was always gruff with Spike, pretending not to approve of his sharing her living quarters, but Shelly knew Gail loved him just as much as she did.

"Go away, dog!" she said in an exasperated voice. "Come on, get your lazy self out to the living room and fall asleep like you always do."

Shelly snickered at the two of them as she sat down at the kitchen table. "He seems like he's got way too much energy for a nap, Gail."

"Ah, don't you be letting him fool you, Shelly girl," Gail said, waving the knife in her hand for emphasis. "Every day after you run, he's always like this up until the time you leave. Then he collapses on the floor and the whole house shakes, and then you can't get him to move the rest of the night." Now she looked at Spike. "Go on, now. Your secret's out. No more trying to impress the girl, you silly animal."

Gail brought her salad to the table and sat down. "Care to join me?" she asked Shelly.

"It looks delicious," Shelly said, "but no. Mom's expecting me for dinner." At first she had found it odd that Gail and Julie had come to live together. Sure, they had several obvious things in common—they were both in their mid-twenties, studying and teaching at Harvard, bright, and attractive—but they had also seemed to have major differences. Julie was a junk-food addict, and Gail was very nutrition conscious. Julie was casual, warm, and open, while Gail was more guarded and reserved.

When Shelly had first met her, Gail had seemed to be outright cold and aloof. At first Shelly had thought she was doing it on purpose, because she thought herself so far above the level of a high school student, but Julie had explained that it was just a defense Gail put up to cope with the stress of dealing with new people and places. Shelly had never thought about it before, but she realized it must feel terribly lonely at first to live in a foreign country among strangers. Going to live in a different state to go to college was scary enough for her. After she had realized this, she had tried hard to make Gail feel more at home, and it had paid off. Once you got to know her, Gail was every bit as warm as Julie.

"So today was the last day of school," Gail said. "How does that feel?"

"Well, it's not really over for good," Shelly said. "College starts in the fall." Then she laughed. "You should know that. You're *still* in school."

"This is true," Gail admitted. "Some of us just don't know when to quit. Are you still set on that school in Colorado?"

Shelly nodded. "I think so."

Gail sighed. "I don't know what it will be like around without our unofficial roommate traipsing in and making things interesting. But you know who's really going to miss you: that great smelly beast passed out in the living room."

Shelly laughed. "Not as much as I'll miss him. But speaking of smelly, I think I better hit the shower."

She left Gail to her dinner, collected her gym bag from the guest room, and headed for the bathroom. The hot water did a lot to restore her energy, and when she came out of the bathroom, her hair still a little damp and stringy, she felt like a new person. She gathered her things and then went to the kitchen to say good-bye to Gail. Shelly was pleasantly surprised to find that Julie had arrived home, and the two of them were sitting at the kitchen table talking.

When Julie saw her, she shot up from the table and hurried over to hug her. "Shelly! No more high school!" she sang. When she released Shelly, she stepped back and swept the long auburn hair out of her eyes, continuing to smile at her radiantly. She had apparently been home long enough to change into a tank top and cut-off sweats. After a few seconds of Julie smiling at her without saying anything, Shelly began to feel weird. She looked to Gail and found that she too wore a secretive grin. Then Gail moved the newspaper on the kitchen table to reveal a little black box with a tiny gold bow and a plain white card on it.

"Happy graduation!" the two of them chorused.

"Oh, you didn't need to get me anything," Shelly said. "Yeah, right," Julie said. She clapped her hands impatiently. "Come on, open it."

"This is an important milestone for you, Shelly," Gail said as she handed her the box. "We wanted to get you something to help you remember it."

Shelly accepted the box and read the card aloud. "To Shelly, from Gail, Julie, and Spike."

They all laughed. Julie said, "Spike picked it out and we paid for it."

Shelly opened the box and found it contained a pair of exquisite blue topaz earrings. "Oh, they're gorgeous!" Shelly exclaimed. After she recovered, she looked up at them and said, "Spike's got excellent taste."

"Well, maybe we helped a little," Julie said.

"I kind of figured that." Shelly picked up one of the tear-drop earrings and let it dangle in her hand to admire it. "These'll look terrific with the dress I got. Thanks, guys. I love them. And I love both of you."

"We love you too," Julie said.

Gail nodded and said, "But if for some reason you don't graduate, you have to give the earrings back."

Shelly had half an hour before she had to leave to get home on time, so she joined Gail and Julie at the table, talking about their students and her graduation plans. She was tempted to tell them about Toby, but she didn't want to sound like she had some silly crush and decided to save it until after she had seen Toby on Friday. Instead she told them all about saving Mrs. Rice from the muggers and the stake-out on Saturday.

Julie found all of this fascinating. After Shelly had finished, she said, "That's one heck of a case your dad's wrapped in now, isn't it?"

Shelly frowned. "What case? What are you talking about?"

"The Back Bay Slayer," Julie said, looking troubled. "I'm sorry. It was in the newspaper, so I assumed you knew about it."

She flipped over the newspaper and showed Shelly the front-page story. The bodies of two women had been found in the Charles River Basin over the last few days, and police believed they had both been the victims of a single killer. The media had dubbed him the Back Bay Slayer, after the Back Bay area on the south side of the river. There was no specific mention that

R. Sherlock Holmes had been brought in as a consultant on the case, but the shadowy black-and-white photo accompanying the story showed him standing among the police officers and men in suits discussing the case in Science Park, the site where the second victim had been found.

"I knew he was working on a pretty disturbing case from the way he's been acting," Shelly said absently, "but he's been very tight-lipped about it."

"Too bad," Julie said. "I'd like a shot at figuring out the mind behind these crimes, but the details in the media so far have been vague."

From anyone else this would have seemed an odd comment, but Julie studied deviant and criminal behavior academically, and serial killers were her specialty. She was full of interesting stories and bits of information, Shelly had come to find. Gail thought they were both terribly morbid when they discussed such things.

"As far as I'm concerned," Gail said now, "the details can stay vague." She shivered. "Talking about crazies and killers like you were talking about a basketball game. You two are not normal, I hope you know that."

Shelly and Julie smiled at each other, as if to say, yes, we know that, and we don't care.

Shelly told Julie, "I'm going to see if I can get my dad to tell me about the case sometime when my mom's not around. On something this big, he probably won't, but if I find out anything, I'll let you know."

Chapter Eight

Shelly reached home just as her mom's Lincoln was pulling into the driveway. Mary Holmes climbed out of the car and called, "Good timing, Shelly. Come here, please. I could use some help."

Shelly followed her mother to the trunk of the car. Mary opened it, revealing a large cardboard box nestled against the spare tire. "It's a lot heavier than it looks," Mary warned as she and Shelly each got a grip on one side of the box and lifted.

"Jeez, Mom, you weren't kidding," Shelly said when the box was balanced on the edge of the trunk. "It feels like it's full of bricks."

"It is," Mary said. "Happy graduation!"

Shelly gave her strange look, and her mother broke down laughing. She seemed almost completely worn out, and her exhaustion was making her giddy. "I'm kidding," Mary said. "It's my latest sculpture. Thanks to your help with the photographs, I finished detailing it today, but it was a lot of work. I just want to get it inside and collapse."

"Ready when you are," Shelly said.

On the count of three, they lifted the box again and carried it to the kitchen door. They rested it on the barbecue grill while Shelly unlocked the door, and then they hauled it inside, staggering a bit and almost losing it before they got it to the kitchen table.

"That's far enough," Mary said, sinking into one of the chairs. "We'll let your father move it to the studio later." Then she looked at Shelly with a conspiratorial smile. "Do you want to see it?"

"You know I do," Shelly replied.

"Get a knife out of the drawer and cut the box away. I just wanted to protect it in the trunk. It'll probably be easier to move without the box anyway."

Shelly got a utility knife and slit the boxtop open and then down each of the four corners so the sides flopped down onto the table, revealing a vague blob swathed in foam packing wrap. Shelly cut the tape holding the wrap in place and then carefully unwound it from around the sculpture.

Mary Holmes's work could be seen in galleries up and down the eastern seaboard, as well as in Los Angeles and London. She worked in a variety of media, though she seemed to be favoring bronze in recent years. Shelly knew her mother thought her best work resulted when she tried to capture and convey her feelings for her family, and this latest piece was obviously such an attempt, and a successful one in Shelly's mind.

It depicted four figures, a mother, father, son, and daughter. They seemed casually arranged at first, but as Shelly studied it she realized that the figures were cleverly positioned so that each of them was touching all of the others. The father had one hand on his son's shoulder, the other casually wrapped around his wife while his daughter touched her lips to his cheek. The mother had one arm around her son, who was holding hands with his sister.

"It's beautiful," Shelly said admiringly. "What are you calling it?"

"*Commitment.*"

"*Commitment,*" Shelly repeated reflectively. "I like it."

"I'll like it more after I've recovered from finishing it," her mother said, rubbing her neck. "I don't feel much like cooking, and your father will be late again, I'm sure. What do you say to ordering a pizza for dinner?"

"I say pepperoni and double cheese."

"You call and I'll pay," her mother offered.

"Deal," Shelly said, already heading for the phone.

Her mother was right; R. Sherlock was late that night. Mary and Shelly watched an old Cary Grant movie on cable, and then her mother went to bed. Shelly didn't have to get up for school the next morning, so she didn't worry about going to bed. She called Amanda and

Kay, and then Maria called her. Then she wrote a short entry in her diary and read the latest issue of *Crime Beat* until her eyelids felt like little invisible people were dragging them down. It was past midnight when she finally gave in, and R. Sherlock had still not returned. Shelly now knew that one of the cases demanding so much of his time involved the Back Bay Slayer. As she drifted off to sleep, she wondered what the other one was about.

Shelly was in that hazy, drifting stage between sleep and waking when she heard someone in the hallway walking past her bedroom door. After years of experience, she could tell her mother's slower, more relaxed gait from her father's heavier, more deliberate footsteps, and this was definitely her father. She sat up in bed and blinked at her clock. It was barely past 5:00 A.M., but her father's footsteps had been going *away* from his bedroom, rather than toward it.

Shelly got out of bed and slipped into her robe. The house was filled with hazy, pre-dawn light, and birds outside seemed to be holding some sort of singing competition. Shelly still wasn't completely awake and almost missed a step going downstairs.

Her father apparently heard the thud as she nearly fell. "Mary?" His resonant voiced carried all the way from the kitchen though he had not spoken loudly.

"No, Dad, it's me," Shelly said, her words partly distorted by an unexpected and irresistible yawn. She reached the kitchen and found him dressed for work and fixing himself a cup of instant coffee. "You're leaving again? I never even heard you get in."

"About four hours ago," he said. "I was careful not to wake anyone. You're up awfully early for school."

She sat down at the kitchen table and pulled her legs up into her robe. There was a slight chill in the air, but that kept her warm. "No school today," she said. "It's a paperwork day for teachers and a make-up day for anyone who missed too many gym classes."

"Is that so?" R. Sherlock murmured, programming the microwave to heat his coffee. When it had come humming to life, seeming very loud so early in the morning, he turned to her and said, "So what are you going to do today?"

"Amanda, Kay, Maria, and I are going to the beach. I'm going to take Spike, too, I think. I want to take some pictures of him trying to catch sea gulls. He's such a goof."

"That sounds like fun," her father said. He seemed somewhat distracted, and the lack of sleep was beginning to have an effect on him. His eyelids seemed a little puffy, and Shelly could see a spot where he had cut himself shaving, a rare occurrence. Shelly pointed this out.

"Sometimes," he said wryly, "it's really annoying to live with someone with a knack for such astute observations. But I encouraged you, so the blame is mine. Yes, I'm a little preoccupied at the moment."

"With the Back Bay Slayer?" Shelly inquired, and then held her breath to await his response.

He closed his eyes and shook his head, chuckling. "How?" was all he said.

"Picture in the paper," Shelly answered. "Julie spotted you."

He nodded. "That explains it. Yes, as a matter of fact, that is a big part of what I've been thinking about. It would be taxing enough without this other case."

"Dad," Shelly said seriously, "I know Mom doesn't want me involved in these kinds of cases and you're just trying to protect me, but if there's any way I can help, I want to. I hate to see you so strung out."

He took her hand and squeezed it. "I appreciate it, sweetheart, but there's really nothing you can do. The second case is pretty much wrapped up an how." He looked back over his shoulder as if he expected his wife to be standing there. "Don't tell your mother I told you any of this, but just to ease your curiosity, here's a rough outline of that case. You know it was a divorce case, which usually involves gathering evidence to prove that one of the parties has been unfaithful to the others. I find the whole thing distasteful myself and never would have taken the case with this Back Bay Slayer on my plate, but it's a little more complicated than that."

He leaned back in his chair and scowled slightly. "Some of the members of our profession don't have much integrity. One such, a real slimy character named Artie Hanks, got involved in this divorce case before me and tried to take advantage of his client. Like I said, I never would have taken this case as busy as I am, but I've had run-ins with Hanks before. He operates in that shadowy area of the law that lets him get away with some pretty unethical behavior. He despises me as much as I do him, and . . . like I said, we've had run-ins in the past. So I took this case to help these people get out from under his thumb, and it looks like I've accomplished that, so I can concentrate on the other case."

"Yeah, it sounds like more than enough," Shelly said. "Two murders."

"Three," her father said quietly, not looking at her. Then his eyes focused on hers. "Don't tell *anyone* you heard that from me. Okay?"

"Of course not, Dad. Have you got any leads?"

The timer on the microwave ran out, and it beeped insistently, once, twice, three times.

Her father wearily pushed himself to his feet.

He smiled at her crookedly. "I think I've let you milk me for enough information for now." He walked over to the microwave.

Rats, Shelly thought. If that thing had waited a little while longer to beep, she might have gotten some real details.

Her father poured the coffee into a travel cup and affixed the lid tightly. "I've got to get going, sweetheart," he said. "Say good morning to your mother for me."

"Sure, Dad," she said. He turned and had reached the back door when she stopped him. "Dad? If things get really busy and you . . . well, if you have to miss my graduation tomorrow, I'll understand."

He smiled back at her, her special smile. "Nothing's going to keep me away tomorrow," he said. "I wouldn't miss it for the world."

He sounded a lot like Kevin when he said those words, but Shelly knew there was one big difference: Her father meant them.

"I love you, Dad."

"I love you, too, sweetheart."

After her father left, Shelly went back to bed. She wasn't about to blow a chance to sleep late, and sleep late she did. When the ringing of the phone on her nightstand startled her awake, she saw that it was almost 10:00 A.M.

"Hello?" she said, ready to grumble at

whomever had dared to disturb her sleep and at the same time trying to make her voice sound bright so whoever it was wouldn't know she had just woken up.

"Hi. Shelly? This is Toby."

She would have sworn her heart stopped right then, and didn't start again until several seconds later when she finally was able to reply. "Hi, Toby. What's up?"

"I was just wondering what time you're planning on showing up at Maria's tomorrow night. I'd really hate to miss you."

"There's not much chance of that," Shelly said. "I'm going over there before the party even starts, to help make sure everything's ready. I'll be watching for you."

"Oh, good, good," he said. "I'm really looking forward to seeing you, Shelly. Ever since we did that chemistry project together . . . well, I like you a lot. I should have told you sooner, but I guess I didn't have the guts."

"Don't worry about it, Toby," she said. "I like you too. I've been trying to figure out how to let you know since that chemistry project, too, and I was just as nervous. I guess it's kind of funny that we were both scared, but the important thing is that now we know how each other feels and we're doing something about it."

"I like the way you think," he said.

Shelly smiled at the compliment, even though

he couldn't see her. She couldn't help it. "Thanks," she said. There was a sort of a pause. Shelly didn't want to hang up yet, but they had pretty much mined out that topic of conversation. The silence stretched on and on, and she could feel herself starting to panic as she tried to think of something else to talk about. Then she came up with the perfect solution. "Hey, Maria and I and a couple of others are going to the beach today. Do you want to go? I'm sure they wouldn't mind."

They'd give her a hard time whenever Toby wasn't looking, Shelly thought, but no, they wouldn't mind.

Toby sounded genuinely sorry. "That sounds like fun," he said, "but I've got to spend the afternoon mowing lawns with my brother. Maybe some other time?"

"Sure," Shelly said. "The summer's just starting."

But what about when summer ended? That seemed like a long way off, but it was only a few months, and then she would be bound for Colorado, leaving Toby and whatever relationship they managed to build up over the summer behind.

Worry about starting the relationship now, she told herself. There would be plenty of time for other worries once they were actually seeing each other on a regular basis.

"Yeah, the summer's just started," he repeated. "And it looks like it's going to be a great one." Then Shelly could hear another voice, a buzzing in the background, and Toby said, "I've got to get going, Shelly. There's a riding lawnmower with my name on it waiting."

Shelly laughed. "Watch out for trees."

"I'll do my best. And I'll see you tomorrow night. Bye."

"Bye."

Shelly hung up and then let herself fall back in her bed so that her head sank into the pillow and her hair flew around her. She lay there for a few more minutes, replaying the phone call in her mind and thinking about what fun she was going to have telling Maria and the others about it.

She waited until they actually got to the beach and had staked out their territory with a motley assortment of lounge chairs and beach towels clustered around a cooler full of canned soft drinks. The sun was bright, the sand was warm, and Spike had cleared the immediate vicinity of everything with wings and feathers. Now he lay panting in the sand next to Shelly's lounge chair. Kay and Amanda were lavishing their attention on him, and he was eating it up.

Maria was talking about the party, reciting from memory the varieties of food that were going to be served. Maria's mom had a flair for parties and didn't fool around when it came to planning one, even if it was just for her daughter and her classmates. The caterer was one of the best in the area.

Then came what Shelly had been waiting for. Kay, in the needling voice she had been using all semester to tease Shelly about Toby, said, "So, Shelly, tell us, are you looking forward to seeing Mr. Ryan tomorrow night?"

Shelly glanced over at her and slid her sunglasses down her nose so Kay could see her eyes. "Why, yes I am, Kay. As a matter of fact that's exactly what I told him when he called me this morning."

Maria shot up faster than when Amanda had dropped the ice cube down the back of her swimsuit. "He called you this morning?" she demanded. "And you didn't tell us?"

Shelly slid her sunglasses back into place and reclined on her lounge chair, smiling hugely. "I guess it just slipped my mind."

"Right," Kay said. "You hit your head in the shower and got amnesia, I suppose." She was the only one not in a bathing suit, because she was naturally very fair skinned and tended to burn easily. She was wearing shorts and an over-size T-shirt, with a big floppy hat covering her long hair. Despite her care to avoid the sun and the liberal layer of sunblock she had smeared on in the car on the way over, the freckles on her face were standing out stronger than ever. "So now that you've miraculously recovered your memory, why don't you tell us why he called?"

"Yeah," Amanda said. "I bet he just needed to know how to find Maria's house."

"Wrong," Shelly announced. "He called," she said slowly, to build suspense, "to find out when exactly I would be at Maria's, because he wanted to make sure he didn't miss me."

"That's what he said?" Kay asked.

"Word for word," Shelly replied.

"That's not a reason to call," Amanda said. "It's an excuse. You know, much as it pains me to say it, I do think the boy's sweet on you, Shell."

"Tell us everything he said," Maria demanded.

The other three girls gathered closer and listened intently as Shelly outlined the conversation for them in as much detail as she could recall. Spike lifted his head from the sand to see where all of his admirers had gone, but after a few seconds he put it down again. Then when Shelly told them what Toby had said about liking her a lot the girls all squealed and howled, and Spike's head shot up once more. Shelly absently petted him to calm him down.

By the time Shelly finished her story, Maria was looking at her like she was the luckiest person on Earth. "You know," Maria said, "tomorrow's probably going to be the biggest day of your life."

Chapter Nine

The day began like any other. Excitement and force of habit combined to make her get up as if she were going to school. She put on sweats and went downstairs to see if her parents had left yet. Her father had actually come home at a decent hour and gone directly to bad. It was the first full night's sleep he had gotten in days, and Shelly was relieved. She had begun to worry about him pushing himself too hard.

She found her parents in the kitchen, talking about their plans to meet Shelly's Uncle Joe and Aunt Tricia for dinner tonight after the graduation ceremony. Her father looked fresh and invigorated, a vast improvement over the previous morning. He looked up from his plate of scrambled eggs as she came in, and winked. She wanted to ask him if there had been any breaks in the Back Bay Slayer case, but she didn't dare with her mother in the room. Mary was dressed up in a smart-looking skirt-suit, though at the moment she was wearing an apron over it while she was cooking.

"Nice outfit, Mom," Shelly said as she took a seat next to her father. "But don't you think it's a little formal for cooking eggs?"

"Very funny," Mary Holmes replied, shoveling fluffy scrambled eggs onto a plate. "I've got an appointment at Boston College this morning," she said. "I'm in the final running to be an artist-in-residence there next year."

"Really?" Shelly said. "That's exciting! Why haven't you said anything before now?" Her mom offered her the plate of scrambled eggs, but Shelly shook her head. Her mother sat down at the table with the plate in front of her.

"Well, I didn't think I had a very good chance because of the competition. I'm a little nervous; it will involve teaching undergraduate courses. Plus I'd be involved in graduate projects, especially those interested in working with bronze.

"That sounds wonderful," Shelly said. Her mom had never shown an interest in teaching before, but maybe that was because she was too busy balancing her time between her own work and raising her kids. Now that Shelly was leaving, there would be that hole in her mother's life that she had been worrying about. Shelly was relieved that her mother seemed to be looking to explore new frontiers in her life, like Shelly would be doing in Colorado, instead of leaving that hole unfilled. Teaching wouldn't fill the hole completely—she would still miss Shelly terribly—but Shelly felt a little easier about leaving home.

"So what are your plans for the day?" her mother asked.

"I'm going to go over to Maria's for some pre-party fun."

"You're not going to get dressed over there, are you?" her mother asked, alarmed.

"No, Mom," Shelly said. "Maria's mom is having the whole thing catered, so there's really nothing for us to do. We'll probably just listen to music and swim in their pool, and I'll be back around noon."

"Good," Mary said. "After all the time we put into finding that dress, I'd like to see you in it. I should be back by lunch, too. If my interview goes well, maybe I'll take you out to celebrate."

"Sounds good," Shelly said.

Her father wiped his mouth on a napkin and stood up, carrying his empty plate. "You ladies have a nice day," he said. "If you'll excuse me, I have to put in some time at the office so I can sneak away to see my little girl graduate high school. I should be back here by…"

"No later than 2:30," Shelly finished the sentence for him.

"I will be home promptly at two," R. Sherlock proclaimed. He kissed his daughter on top of the head. "Good luck," he whispered to his wife and then kissed her as well.

Shelly's mom left for her interview a few minutes later, and then Shelly ran upstairs to get ready to go to Maria's.

Shelly spent the morning with her friends, splashing in the pool and trying to work off some of the nervous energy generated by their anticipation of the graduation ceremony this afternoon and the party afterward. It didn't work, but they had a terrific time. They split up to go home for lunch, and pledged to meet each other when they got to school for graduation.

When Shelly reached home, she found her mother in excellent spirits. The artist-in-residence candidates had been whittled down to two, Mary Holmes and one other, and Mary said the interview had gone fabulously. She took Shelly to lunch at an open-air cafe and told her all about the campus, how beautiful it was, how nice the faculty, how conveniently located to their home. By the end of lunch, Shelly joked that her mom had painted such an attractive picture she thinking of going there instead of the University of Colorado.

When they got home, they started getting ready for the big event together. They curled each others hair, and Mary did Shelly's nails for her. They got to laughing so hard while they were at it, Mary nearly got strawberry gloss nail polish on Shelly's fingers instead of her nails. Precisely at 2:00, R. Sherlock arrived home and found them giggling helplessly.

"Right on time, Dad," Shelly gasped between giggles.

R. Sherlock regarded them expressionlessly for a few moments and then said. "Mary, would you mind doing my nails, when you've finished Shelly's? I think that shade would look terrific with my gray suit."

Then he walked away down the hall leaving his wife and daughter doubled up with new laughter behind him. After another few minutes, they began to recover and compose themselves. Shelly walked around the house blowing on her nails to hurry their drying while her mother went to get dressed. When her nails had finally dried, Shelly went to her room and slipped into the dress she and her mom had found together. After she ran through her mental checklist—hair, face, nails, dress, shoes—she turned to the full-length mirror on the back of her door to check out the full effect. She smiled and turned for a side view. Yes, she decided, pleased: It had been worth all the trouble.

She opened her bedroom door, ready to strike a pose for her parents' appreciation, but the upstairs area was quiet. Puzzled, she went downstairs. She didn't hear them anywhere. They weren't in the kitchen.

Then she heard Eric Clapton's "Wonderful Tonight," one of her father's favorite songs, begin to play from the living room. She walked down the hall to the open entryway and found her parents standing there looking proud and misty and secretive all at once. When Mary saw her daughter, she smiled and opened her mouth but said nothing. Shelly was sure she was going to start crying any second. Her father's jaw dropped when he first saw her, and he blinked a couple of times. Then he was sweeping across the floor toward her.

"May I have this dance?" he said, bowing gallantly.

"Dad, sometimes you're so corny," she said, but she took his hand and danced with him, feeling that she might start crying herself. Mary watched them glide gracefully around the room with her hands held tightly in front of her. Shelly smiled at her each time they passed.

When the song ended, her dad stopped the CD player and turned back to Shelly with a small jewelry box in the palm of his hand. "Your mother and I have something for you," he said.

"We were going to get you something practical for college," Mary said, talking quickly in her excitement, "but we figured your birthday is in August and that we could get you something practical then. So we got you something special."

Shelly accepted the box from her father and opened it. A small diamond heart necklace glittered on its little satin bed.

"Oh my gosh!" Shelly said. "It's beautiful."

She carefully removed it from the box and

then looked to her father for help. He took the pendant, and while Shelly held her hair up away from her neck, he stood behind her and fastened it in place.

Shelly admired it in the mirror and then turned back to her parents. "I love it. Thank you," she said and then kissed each of them.

"Don't move," her mother said, hurrying from the room. "I've got to get my camera."

After she was gone, R. Sherlock took out his wallet and slipped Shelly a twenty-dollar bill. "Emergency money," he said.

"Thanks, Dad."

Then Mary returned with her camera and they spent several minutes taking pictures in different combinations: Shelly alone, Shelly with her father, R. Sherlock and Mary together looking proud. Then R. Sherlock started clowning around taking a picture of Shelly and her mother, holding the camera backward and flashing himself.

"Don't get me started laughing again, Dad," Shelly scolded him with a smile. "My makeup's going to run and I'll go through graduation looking like a raccoon."

"And we'd be very proud of our little raccoon, wouldn't we, Mary?" her father said.

"Whatever you say, dear, but it's time we should be going."

Time to go. Shelly started feeling the excitement fluttering in her stomach. It was time to graduate.

They met up with Mr. and Mrs. Dunn in the high school parking lot, but after an exchange of greetings and compliments on how nice everyone looked, Shelly had to leave them to find their seats while she went in to join the other seniors. The lunchroom, where they were all putting on their caps and gowns, was littered with white cardboard boxes and tissue paper.

Shelly found her friends gathered around one table and had a chance to show off her new pendant before she too put on her cap and gown. Then they chatted excitedly until Mr. Thorne came in clapping his hands for attention to get them lined up.

The ceremony itself seemed somehow unreal to Shelly, like a dream. As they filed into the auditorium, packed with people in suits and dresses, she felt almost as if she were floating. Her eyes swept the assembled faces focused on the seniors, but she didn't see her parents or the Dunns.

Joanne's valedictory address and the other formalities flew by for Shelly, as she spent the time scanning the crowd for familiar faces. There were so many people, she was not too surprised that she still couldn't find her parents and the Dunns.

Then Principal Hawkins began to call names, and Shelly became entranced watching each of her classmates negotiate their way down the risers, careful in their flowing gowns, to shake Principal Hawkins's hand and accept their diploma with a triumphant grin. As they went through the class alphabetically, Amanda Blaine was the first of Shelly's friends to be called. Shelly applauded and shouted, "Go, Amanda!" though she could scarcely be heard over the crowd. She did the same when Kay Delaney was called shortly thereafter, and then she settled down for the nervous countdown to her name.

"Shelly Elizabeth Holmes," Principal Hawkins called, and Shelly found she liked the sound of her name reverberating around the huge auditorium. She picked her way to the aisle and descended the risers to reach the podium. On her way, the flash of a camera caught her eye, and spotting its source, she saw her mom sitting tall next to her father and Mr. and Mrs. Dunn. Shelly gave a tiny wave in their direction, and Mary's camera flashed again, as it did a few seconds later when Principal Hawkins presented her with her diploma and shook her hand. Then she was heading back to her seat, her diploma clutched in both hands. She didn't pay much attention to the rest of the ceremony, except when Maria was called and she contributed to the shouts and applause—and of course Shelly saved one last scream of joy for Toby Ryan.

Finally, the huge stack of diplomas was exhausted, and Principal Hawkins presented the graduates to the audience. Amidst the deafening uproar that ensued, the seniors all stood and tossed their caps into the air. Then the band was playing again, and they began to file out of the auditorium, everyone looking happy and proud, with a few of the bigger class clowns doing little dance steps as they exited.

Shelly found her friends and exchanged congratulatory hugs. Then excited relatives began mingling with the graduates, and pandemonium seemed to reign throughout the school for a while. Shelly had to stand on a chair and scan the crowd from a higher vantage point to locate her parents and the Dunns, who spotted her and waved. They squeezed through the crowd and exchanged hugs and happy words. Shelly thought she'd never been hugged so many times in one day in her life.

And then it was time to leave. It seemed kind of abrupt to Shelly, and she was a little surprised that she was sorry to see it end. Her parents told her to enjoy Maria's party, and then they were gone. Shelly went back to the lunchroom, where Maria and Kay had already changed out of their gowns.

Shelly threw off her own gown and said, "It's party time!"

Shelly drove Maria, Kay, and Amanda to Maria's house in her mother's Lincoln. As they had lingered at the high school, wishing everyone a good summer and good luck with the future, Maria's parents had beat them home by a good half hour. The caterers had arrived and had everything well in hand, moving the furniture to create clear areas in all of the first-floor rooms of the house and erecting long buffet tables.

Sammie Slam, a local DJ who had graduated from their high school several years ago, showed up with his gear and began setting up in the huge family room, which had a high ceiling crossed with heavy timbers and glass doors leading out onto the patio.

There really was not much for the girls to do, which was fine with them. They wandered from room to room on the first floor—the upstairs area was off-limits—watching the caterers set up, sneaking tastes in the kitchen, looking through Sammie Slam's musical selection. And they talked.

"Did Toby say what time he'll be here?" Kay asked when they were out on the patio, admiring the way the setting sun glimmered on the surface of the lake that lapped at the edge of the backyard.

"No," Shelly said. She shook her hands in front of her to loosen them up. "And I'm really starting to get nervous."

"Shelly," Amanda said, "just relax. He already said he likes you. What have you got to be nervous about?"

"What are we going to talk about?" she asked. "We had to practice for an hour so I could ask him if he was coming to this party, and now I don't even have that."

"Just ask him about himself," Maria said with authority. "Boys love to talk about themselves."

"So true," Kay and Amanda chorused.

Shelly laughed.

"And if he's one of the rare exceptions," Kay said, "you've got plenty to talk about. You're one of the most interesting people I've ever met. Tell him about Spike and Julie and Gail. Or tell him about going on the stakeout with your dad. Or talk about photography."

Shelly put her hand on Kay's shoulder. "Thanks," she said. Then she looked at the others. "All of you. It's because of you I've gotten this far, and with your support I know I'll do okay."

The others nodded.

Amanda said, "Just don't blow it," and they all broke up laughing.

The guests started arriving soon after that, and the four of them took turns greeting people and showing them around. When there were a few guests gathered in the family room, Sammie

Slam started rocking and it really started to feel like a party. The place filled up quickly after that.

Shelly was standing at the door with Maria and Amanda when Toby arrived. He was wearing black jeans with a steely gray sportcoat over a red T-shirt. She heard Maria whistle quietly, and Amanda winked at her. She had to admit, he looked absolutely gorgeous tonight.

"Hi, Toby," she said with a small wave.

"Wow, Shelly," he said appreciatively, "you look terrific."

"Thanks. You're looking pretty sharp yourself. Come on, I'll show you around."

Shelly took him by the hand and gave him a little tour of Maria's house. They stopped to talk with a few people they knew, and then they strolled along the buffet tables together and filled plates with delicious little pastries and shrimp salad sandwiches, stuffed mushrooms, fresh veggies and dip, and all sorts of other tempting morsels.

They laughed and talked as they ate on chairs set up in the dining room, out of the way of the mainstream of the party. Her friends had been right; now that Toby was here she had no problem talking to him. They talked about books and movies, their parents and other relatives, basketball, the best way to cook hot dogs, and how to develop film. In fact, they ended up talking until almost everyone else had started to leave.

It wasn't until Shelly saw Amanda and Kay stroll past the dining room entrance, glancing in casually as they passed, as if they didn't know she and Toby were in there, that she thought of the time. She locked at her watch.

"Oh my gosh!" she said, truly startled. "It's past midnight."

"You're kidding," Toby said, checking his own watch for confirmation. "No, I guess you're not. Were you supposed to be home by midnight?"

"No, it's just that I'm giving a ride to Kay and Amanda, and I've seen them checking up on us."

Toby laughed. "Yeah, I understand. I should be getting home myself." They stood, and Toby took both of Shelly's hands in his. "I really had a great time," he said. "I hope I can see you again soon."

"I don't have a problem with that," Shelly said playfully. "Call me anytime. Or maybe I'll call you first."

Toby was nodding. "Cool. Well, good night."

He kissed her. "Good night," Shelly called softly after him as he left.

As soon as he was out of sight, Amanda and Kay were in the room begging for details. They said good night to Maria, who was in love again, with someone she had met tonight, and then in the car Shelly gave them all the details they could want.

After she had dropped them off at their houses and Shelly was alone in the car, she had time to reflect on what a perfect evening it had been. She realized now that though she had had a crush on Toby for months, she had hardly known him. Now that she knew him better, she liked him even more.

When she got home, though, thoughts of Toby vanished from her mind. Her father's car was not parked in the driveway, but Julie's Range Rover was. Shelly couldn't imagine what Julie would be doing here at this time of night.

Shelly's headlights picked Julie out of the darkness. She had apparently been sitting on the back steps, but now she stood and came around the Lincoln.

Shelly got out and asked, "Julie, what's going on?"

Julie looked pale and shaken. She put her hand on Shelly's arm. She said, "Shelly, it's your parents. There's . . . there's been an accident."

Chapter Ten

"What kind of accident?" Shelly demanded. To go from feeling so utterly happy to so coldly frightened was the most horrible feeling she had ever experienced. "Are they okay?"

"I don't know the details," Julie said. She was speaking slowly and calmly, but Shelly could tell it was an effort for her. "Your aunt called me from the emergency room and asked for my help finding you."

"What happened?" Shelly asked. She felt like she might start crying at any moment.

"All your aunt told me was that your parents left her house and had a car accident on their way home. This was about an hour ago."

A mistake, Shelly thought. It was a big mistake. Her father was a terrific driver. Someone must have made a mistake. "Are they sure it's my parents?" she asked, but deep inside her she already knew the answer.

"I'm afraid so," Julie said.

Thoughts and worries swam so thickly through her head, all Shelly could think of to say was "They had dinner together."

"Who did?" Julie asked with a confused frown.

"My parents and my aunt and uncle."

Julie nodded and put her arm around Shelly. "Come on," she said, guiding Shelly to the Range Rover's passenger door. "I'll take you to the hospital, and we can find out what's going on."

The ride was a slow and seemingly endless torture. She and Julie didn't speak. Shelly knew if she started talking she was going to break down, and she supposed there wasn't really anything else for Julie to say. She watched distant lights stretched out to the horizon as Julie guided the Range Rover along the dark highway. Shelly started to shiver slightly, and goose bumps rose on her bare arms. She had a wild thought that if she had gotten the type of long-sleeved dress her mother had favored, she would be warm right now. She thought of the shopping trips with her mom. They had had their share of frustration and disagreements, but Shelly had loved going shopping with her mom. The thought that she might never get to do it again...it was just too unbearable to think about.

The ride seemed to last forever, but when they finally drew within sight of the hospital, Shelly began to feel a new dread growing within her. The tall building was well lit, and even at this hour there was a lot of activity. The flashing lights of an ambulance strobed at the emergency entrance. Shelly didn't want to go near the place. She had the unrealistic feeling that if she didn't go in and find out what was going on, her parents would be all right. As long as no one told her otherwise, they would be fine.

But she knew how foolish that was, and despite the mounting fear inside her she maintained her composure after Julie parked the Range Rover and they started the long trek to the building from the parking lot. They still did not speak. Shelly listened to the sharp clicking of her heels on the asphalt, such a clear sound in the stillness of the night, and tried to ignore the dreadful feeling inside her.

Inside the hospital it was worse. The darkness outside had been somehow comforting, but inside all was starkly bright under the buzzing fluorescent lights. The corridor echoed with the distant din of the emergency room, and the antiseptic smell was sharp in Shelly's nostrils.

Julie had been guiding her, but suddenly seemed unsure of herself. "This is the right place," she murmured. Then she spotted a nurses' station. "Hold on. I'll ask about them over here."

"No, wait," Shelly said, her attention focused down a different hallway. She started walking in that direction. It led into a waiting room, with ocean-blue carpeting and windows overlooking the parking lot. "I see my aunt."

Tricia Holmes was sitting, head slightly bowed, on a black vinyl sofa. As Shelly numbly walked down the hallway toward the waiting room, Julie at her side, she saw her aunt remove her glasses and run a hand through her inky black hair. Shelly had never before seen her Aunt Tricia cry, but she saw her crying now.

As Shelly got closer, her Uncle Joe came into view, sitting next to his wife. He was leaning all the way against the back of the couch, one hand absently rubbing his chin as if he were pondering some deep accounting matter. Only he didn't look like he was thinking about his business at the moment. His expression was somber, and his eyes, turned upward and unfocused, shone with unreleased tears. Joe Holmes, her father's brother, resembled R. Sherlock to a remarkable degree. Though he was heavier, and his hair had begun to fall out on top, Shelly could make out the sharp angles of her father's face in Uncle Joe's softer one, and the gray eyes were the same. It was Uncle Joe who noticed Shelly first.

He struggled to rise to meet her, and Aunt Tricia looked up in surprise. Shelly rushed the last few steps to reach them. There was nobody else in the waiting room.

"Uncle Joe," she said, aware of a half-hysterical edge in her voice and not caring, "where are my parents?"

His mouth opened. He licked his lips and closed it again.

"Oh, Shelly!" her Aunt Tricia cried. She had

risen with her husband and now threw her arms around Shelly. Shelly could feel her trembling. "I'm so sorry. Your dad is in surgery, and your mom . . . she didn't make it."

"Didn't make it?" Shelly repeated angrily. "What do you mean she 'didn't make it?'"

Shelly felt Julie's reassuring hand on her back and glanced behind her to see the flood of tears in Julie's eyes.

"I'm sorry," her aunt said, releasing her. "There was nothing the doctors could do."

"My mother is *dead*?" Shelly asked. She can't be dead, Shelly wanted to say. I just saw her tonight. She was at my graduation, smiling and taking pictures. "She can't be," Shelly heard herself say.

"Shelly, why don't you have a seat," her uncle said. "Julie, maybe you could get us a glass of water."

"No!" Shelly shouted. "I don't want anything to drink." She reached back blindly and groped for Julie's hand. Julie took Shelly's hand and squeezed it reassuringly. "I want to see my dad," Shelly said, more levelly now.

"He's in surgery," her uncle explained gently. "The doctors are trying to save his life. After he comes out of surgery and the doctors have something to tell us, they'll come here and find us. Until then there's nothing we can do but sit and wait."

Shelly wanted to blow up at him and yell and scream until she couldn't anymore. She wanted to yell and scream at anyone, and Uncle Joe was the most immediate target, but the pain in his eyes was like a mirror of her own, and she realized that this was just as hard on him as it was on herself. She decided not to make it any harder. Still holding Julie's hand, she went to the sofa perpendicular to the one where her aunt and uncle had been sitting, and she sat down. Julie followed her without a word, and after a moment her aunt and uncle returned to the places they had occupied before Shelly's arrival.

Silence held sway in the otherwise empty waiting room except for the faint sounds of distant activity elsewhere in the hospital, funneled through the gleaming white corridors. Shelly stared at a cigarette burn on the ocean-blue carpet and tried to come to grips with the reality of never seeing her mother again.

After a few minutes, she asked, "How did it happen?" without looking up from carpet.

Uncle Joe cleared his throat. "After dinner tonight, we stopped back at our house for a cup of coffee."

"I showed your mom the new computer we just bought for Russell," Aunt Tricia said, pausing to dab at her eyes with a tissue. "She said it was the same one they were going to get you for college."

"They left around 10:00, maybe 10:15," Uncle Joe continued. "We were just settling down to watch the news when the doorbell rang. Two police officers were standing there. The light on their car was flashing. They told me your parents had been involved in an automobile accident with another driver. Your father had been identified, and someone among the police had known to contact me. They told us which hospital your parents had been taken to, and we came right here."

"As soon as we found out their condition," Aunt Tricia said, "we tried to call you at home. Your mother had mentioned you would be out late at a party at a friend's house, but we had no idea where. So we called Julie. She didn't know where the party was either, but she volunteered to wait at your house and bring you when you got home. Thanks again, Julie."

Julie nodded but did not speak. Shelly squeezed her hand.

"I did manage to reach your brother Kevin," Uncle Joe said. "He said he would be on the next plane."

Shelly fought the urge to make a bitter comment about him missing rehearsal for his play. Kevin could be insensitive and self-centered at times—most of the time—but he could be compassionate and caring when circumstances were serious enough. Shelly couldn't think of any circumstances more serious than this.

"Do you think my dad will be okay?" Shelly asked.

"I don't know," Uncle Joe answered softly. "I hope so."

Time crawled past after that. Aunt Tricia offered to get Shelly something to eat or drink from the cafeteria, but she had no appetite. Her stomach felt like it had been wrung out like a damp towel. She stared at the carpet or at lights outside the window. Nothing seemed to change for hours.

Finally, though she did not want to leave in case the doctors should come while she was gone, she admitted to herself that she had to go to the bathroom. She asked her aunt if she knew were the ladies' room was.

"Down the hallway here," her aunt pointed.

"Thanks."

Julie rose with Shelly and said, "I'll go with you."

They walked down the corridor together, past a drinking fountain and a blank-faced fire door.

"I feel like my heart's been ripped out," Shelly said.

"I know," Julie said. "And this waiting is awful."

"As long as it turns out all right," Shelly said, "I don't mind. I'll wait all night, as long as the doctor comes in and says my dad's going to be okay."

"Me too," Julie said.

After they visited the rest room, they stopped at the drinking fountain. Only when the water was sliding its cool way down her throat did Shelly realize how thirsty she had been. When they returned to the waiting room, it was just as they had left it. No one said anything as Shelly and Julie returned to their seats and resumed waiting.

It was not long after that that a tall man dressed in hospital greens looked inquiringly into the room. He was balding, and what hair he did have was shaved close to his head. "Holmes family?" he asked.

They all stood at once. "Yes," Uncle Joe said.

"I'm Dr. Prager," the tall man said, "the attending surgeon. I'm very sorry. We did everything we could."

At first no one said anything. Then Uncle Joe, sounding very professional, said, "I understand, doctor. How do we proceed?"

"Why don't you come with me?" he said, scanning the grief-stricken faces around him. There was concern in his eyes, but he seemed to be all business. He led Uncle Joe back the way he had come. As they talked in low voices, Shelly heard the doctor ask, "How were you related to the deceased?"

Shelly's mind stuck on the word *deceased*. It

was like a dagger driven through her heart, and her face tightened in pain, as if she had been physically wounded. It was too much. This morning she had been happy and hopeful, and then tonight she had suddenly lost both of her parents. She had never felt so alone in her life. She sank back onto the sofa and buried her face in her hands, sobbing uncontrollably. She felt Julie's arm patting her softly on the back, and that was all she noticed of the world surrounding her for several minutes.

When she finally looked up again, feeling an exhaustion deeper than any she had ever known, her aunt was ready to offer her a tissue. She accepted it, but could not keep from trembling as she cleaned up her face. The tissue came away blackened by mascara. Her makeup was running. *We'd be very proud of our little raccoon,* her father's voice echoed in her mind.

"Shelly," her aunt said, and then repeated more sharply to get her attention, "Shelly, it's going to be all right. Why don't you come home with us tonight? Your Uncle Joe will take care of all the arrangements."

"No," Shelly said, shaking her head vigorously.

"Shelly, I think—"

"No!" Shelly repeated, not sure where her determination was coming from. "I want to go home. That's where Kevin will go."

"We can call Kevin from our house," Aunt Tricia said. "You should be around people."

"I want to go home."

"I'll go with her and spend the night," Julie said.

Aunt Tricia looked like she wanted to keep trying to persuade Shelly, but she gave in. "I'll call to see how you're doing in the morning," she finally said.

Shelly thanked her aunt, and then she and Julie left the waiting room. She was very grateful to have Julie as a guide to show her the way out of the hospital. And as a friend.

"Thanks for staying with me, Julie," she said during the walk back across the parking lot. "I don't know how I'd get through this without you."

"It's okay, Shelly," her friend answered. "I'm here whenever you need me, for anything. Would you rather stay at my place, with Gail and Spike?"

It was a tempting offer, but Shelly felt for some reason that she needed to stay in her own house. She didn't really understand why, but Julie accepted this with no further explanation.

They drove back to Shelly's house without speaking. When they arrived, the Lincoln parked in the driveway made Shelly remember Maria's party and the time she had spent with Toby. She was so happy then. She never would have believed she could be so emotionally devastated only a few hours later. She wished the entire night had never happened.

When they went inside, Julie asked, "Do you want to have a cup of tea or something to eat?"

"No," Shelly said softly. "I just need time to deal with this. I still can't believe I'll never see them again."

"I know. It's a terrible, terrible thing."

Shelly nodded. "Do you know where the guest room is?"

"Yes," Julie replied. "I'll be fine. Don't worry about me. You just let me know if there's anything I can do for you. Any time. Promise?"

Shelly actually managed a weak smile, the first one since she had left Maria's. "I promise," she said. Then she went to her father's study and closed the door. She curled up on the leather sofa and cried softly until she finally fell asleep.

Chapter Eleven

Shelly woke the next morning with the feeling she'd had an awful nightmare. When she opened her eyes and saw she was in the study, all of last night's events came back at once, bringing with them a fresh wave of grief and that terrible feeling of being alone in the world. When she moved to sit up she found her body was stiff and achy from her strange sleeping accommodations, but it was still nothing compared with the way she felt inside. She left the study and found Julie in the kitchen eating blueberry waffles cooked in the toaster.

Julie blinked at her once when she saw the way Shelly looked, still in her graduation dress. Julie was being too careful of Shelly's emotions to say anything, but Shelly realized she must look terrible. She found she didn't much care, either.

"Morning," Shelly said.

"Good morning. How are you feeling?"

"Like I might crumble into a million pieces at any moment." The smell of Julie's waffles made Shelly realize with vague surprise that her appetite was coming back with a vengeance. She walked to the freezer to see if there were any more waffles. "Has my aunt called yet this morning?"

Julie nodded. "I told her you were still sleeping, and I didn't want to wake you. Kevin called too."

Shelly looked back at Julie, the freezer door held open. "Where is he?"

"He's probably getting into the airport right about now. He got delayed last night."

"Figures," Shelly muttered as she pulled the box of waffles out of the freezer.

"Your uncle is picking him up, and they're all going to come over here around noon."

Shelly nodded. That would give her time to pull herself together before she had to go and face other people. She was relieved about that.

"Oh, your aunt also said to let you know she contacted your Aunt Eileen for you."

That surprised Shelly. Aunt Eileen was her mother's sister, and Shelly didn't think Aunt Tricia had ever met her since she lived in London. Maybe they met at her parents' wedding, Shelly thought. She pushed two waffles down in the toaster just as the phone began to ring in the hallway. Julie started to rise, but Shelly waved her back in her seat and said, "I'll get it."

She picked up the phone. "Hello?"

"Hi, Shelly. It's Toby. Is it true?"

"Is what true?" she asked. Hearing his voice confused her in an odd way. It seemed that he belonged in a different world, a happy world in which her parents were still alive.

"That your parents . . . I heard they had a car accident last night."

"How did you know?" Shelly asked.

"It's true," he said grimly. "I'm so sorry, Shelly. Things must be pretty tough for you right now. I just wanted to let you know that if you needed anything, even just someone to talk to, I'm here."

"Thanks, Toby. I'm just trying to hold myself together at the moment. I'll talk to you later."

"Okay, Shelly. Take care."

She hung up quickly before she started to cry again. When she went back into the kitchen, Julie asked, "Who was that?"

"A friend from high school. He called to offer condolences. I wonder how he knew?"

Julie flipped over a newspaper on the kitchen table. The headline read WORLD-FAMOUS DETECTIVE KILLED IN CAR CRASH.

Shelly stepped closer. "Are the police investigating? It might not have been an accident. My dad was involved in cases against some pretty shady characters...."

Julie was shaking her head. "Shelly, the other driver was an eighteen-year-old high school student. He was driving home from a graduation party where there had been a lot of drinking going on. Your aunt said the test results haven't confirmed it yet, but everyone's pretty sure he was drunk."

"How ironic," Shelly said, without feeling.

"What do you mean?" Julie asked.

"My parents don't—didn't—drink alcohol. Nobody in my family does. And they were killed by a drunk driver."

Shelly's waffles popped up in the toaster, and the phone started ringing again. "Eat your breakfast," Julie said. "I'll get this one."

As Shelly spread butter and syrup on her waffles, she heard Julie speaking on the phone. She was trying to keep her voice low, but Shelly could tell she was angry about something.

"Who was that?" Shelly asked when Julie returned a few moments later.

"No one. Just some guy."

"What did he want?" Shelly asked. When Julie hesitated, she said, "I can handle this, Julie."

Julie nodded. "Okay. He was a business broker. Apparently he read the newspaper this morning too. He wanted to know if you would let him handle the sale of your father's detective agency."

"Sell the agency?" Shelly said. The notion hadn't occurred to her, but now that someone else had suggested it, she found it . . . insulting. "Never."

"Well, that guy's an insensitive vulture, sure,"

Julie said, "but aren't you going to sell it? Without your father, it's just a name and an office. You couldn't run it from Colorado, and Kevin will probably want to sell it. The vulture said that based on the name you could expect a good price."

"I don't care about the money, and I don't care what Kevin thinks," Shelly said, but then she looked doubtful. "But I don't know what else I can do. I just can't bear the thought of selling it."

"Listen, you don't have to worry about any of this now. There'll be plenty of time to think about it. How about after you finish breakfast we go take Spike for a walk?"

"Yeah," Shelly said. "I think I'd like that."

When they returned, Shelly was still feeling less than herself, but Spike's clumsy affection had done a lot to cheer her up. She had finally changed out of her graduation dress and taken a long shower at Julie's apartment, and she felt like she could hold herself together to face other people and her responsibilities. This was fortunate, because when Julie's Range Rover reached Shelly's house again they found cars filling the driveway and lining the street in front. A number of reporters were gathered on the front lawn.

Julie looked uneasy. "Do you feel up to trying to get past them?" she asked.

Shelly thought about it for a moment and nodded. "They probably know Dad had a daughter, but they probably don't know what I look like. They probably think I'm already inside. I see several of my friends' cars, so as long as we don't run or look like we've got a reason to dodge them they'll just think we're friends coming to pay our respects."

Julie still looked unsure, but she said, "Okay, if you say so."

They got out of the Range Rover and strolled leisurely up the driveway. Several of the reporters looked over in their direction. "You relatives?" one called, who was standing with his camera crew.

Shelly shook her head. "Friends of Shelly's."

The reporters went back to talking to one another and ignored them.

When they reached the front door, Julie said, "Sometimes you're so clever it's spooky," she whispered.

"Family tradition," Shelly said, wishing she were in a better mood so she could appreciate the compliment.

They went inside. Shelly was surprised to spot Toby in the living room talking to Amanda and Kay. Amanda saw her and waved. The others turned. They all looked grim and subdued, but also concerned. Shelly was glad they were there.

"I'm going to find your aunt," Julie said. "Why don't you go talk to your friends, and I'll let her know that you're here."

"All right." She went into the living room and said hi. Each of them in turn hugged her and told her how sorry they were. Toby was last. Hugging him wasn't as awkward as she had expected.

"The reporters out front didn't give you trouble, did they?" he asked. The protectiveness in his voice made her smile a little.

"No," she said, and she explained how they had walked right past them.

"That's our Shelly," Kay said.

"I've got to go look for my brother," Shelly said. "I haven't seen him yet."

"I saw him earlier," Amanda said. "I think he's in the study with your uncle."

"Thanks. I'll see you in a little bit."

Shelly went down the hallway to her father's study and found the door almost closed. The mention of her name made her pause before entering.

"I'm really busy; most days I don't get home until after midnight," came Kevin's voice, as resonant as her father's, though a bit higher and more expressive. "Shelly would be all alone in New York."

"I know," said a voice she recognized as her Uncle Joe's. "Your aunt and I have talked it over and think she should come stay with us until she leaves for college in the fall."

"That would probably be for the best," Kevin agreed.

"As for the will, I've been in contact with Stephen Baker, your parents' attorney, and the reading will have to wait until Tuesday."

"Tuesday?" Kevin said. "I can't wait around until Tuesday. We open on Friday. Isn't there any way we can do it earlier?"

"I'm afraid not. Mr. Baker said that part of the will is a videotaped message from your parents. Only one copy of the videotape exists, and it's stored in a safe deposit box downtown. The bank has already closed for today, tomorrow's Sunday, and Monday is Memorial Day. He won't be able to retrieve the videotape until Tuesday morning at the earliest. New York isn't far by plane. Perhaps you can fly back in the meantime and return for the reading."

"I guess I'll have to," Kevin said. "A videotape, huh? I wonder what that's all about."

"I haven't any idea. I'm not privy to the details of the will, but as your father's accountant I know the estate is sizable, including the house. If you need any financial help in the meantime—"

"No, that's okay," Kevin said. "New York is expensive, but I make over a hundred grand a year."

"Really?" Uncle Joe said sounding startled. "I had no idea acting was so lucrative."

"Most of the time it's not, but when you're working regularly—yeah, it's all right. I've been pretty lucky. You should be more concerned about Shelly. Will her share get her though college comfortably?"

"I would expect so. And you can always sell the agency. The name means a lot in professional circles, and I'm certain there are many people who would pay a good price for it."

That was more than Shelly could bear. She was in the room before she could stop herself. "I apologize for eavesdropping," she said, nothing in the harsh tones of her voice suggesting she was truly sorry, "but I would appreciate it if you would include me in any plans for my own future. I'm going to be eighteen in a few months, a legal adult, and I—"

"Calm down, Shelly," Kevin said as he stood and hugged her, so strongly that her feet left the floor. "We were just talking through options. If we had known you were playing detective outside the door we would have invited you in."

She looked at the concern on his face and realized how much she had missed him. Then she burst into tears. "Mom and Dad are dead," she said, sobbing into his shoulder.

"I know," he said consolingly. "I know."

Uncle Joe slipped discreetly from the room,

and left them alone to share their grief.

The rest of the day was a trying chaos of friends, relatives, and funeral arrangements. Aunt Eileen was unable to reschedule her meetings. She worked for the Prime Minister, and the decision was made not to delay the services. Uncle Joe issued a brief statement to the press on behalf of the family that finally cleared the yard of reporters. The network of activity was the kitchen. Aunt Tricia kept a constant supply of refreshments ready for visitors who came by to pay their respects.

Shelly remained in the thick of things for as long as she could stand it, but late that afternoon, after her friends had left and the living room had filled with friends of her parents—mostly policemen and artists and other professionals they knew through their respective careers—she finally fled upstairs for a little solitude. She started to catch her diary up to the present, but she just couldn't bring herself to write down what had happened. It was still too painful. She closed her diary on the blank page and was capping her pen when Kevin found her.

"Hi," he said, knocking on the frame of the open door. "Mind a little company?"

"No," Shelly said. "Not yours anyway."

He gave her an understanding smile. "It's kind of a circus down there, isn't it?"

"Yeah," Shelly said. "I thought you liked that kind of thing."

He shrugged. "Under other circumstances, yeah. Listen, Shelly, I wanted to apologize about not coming to your graduation yesterday."

"It's okay," she said, thinking they'd already covered this on the phone.

"No, it's not okay," he said. "You forgive me too easily sometimes, Shelly, and I take advantage of it. I promised I would be there, and I should've been there. It was a crummy thing to do. I can't change it, but I am sorry."

Talk of graduation made Shelly think about her diploma. She had given it to her mother after the ceremony to bring home and had not seen it since. She had only been here in her room once, briefly, to change out of her dress, and now she thought to look around for her diploma to show it to Kevin. She spotted it on her desk by the window, and next to it, a stack of photographs.

She pushed herself off her bed and went to the desk. The top photograph showed her admiring her graduation present pendant around her neck while her father stood grinning next to her. They were the pictures her mother had taken yesterday.

"Maybe," she said, looking up at Kevin, smiling and crying at the same time, "you can still be there."

She took the stack of photos over and sat next to him on her bed. One by one, she took him through the photographs of her dancing with her father and clowning with her mother beforehand, of her waving as she walked to the podium to receive her diploma, of all three of them afterward in a photo kindly taken by Mr. Dunn. It took nearly half an hour with Shelly filling in all of the details, and by the end both of them had tears streaking their faces.

Kevin kissed her on the cheek. "I wish I had kept my promise to you," he said, and he hugged her.

Chapter Twelve

Sunday, the day of the funeral, was a gray and overcast day that threatened rain throughout the service and never delivered. Shelly had never seen so many flowers in her life, forming thick barriers around the twin caskets, but in the grayness of the day even the flowers looked cheerless.

When the service finally ended, the somber crowd began to disperse through the cemetery, back to their cars. Shelly lingered, considering the location of her parents' final resting place. They had bought their plots several years ago, it turned out, though Shelly had known nothing about them. They overlooked a grassy slope that ended at the edge of a steep ravine. Across that, the thick woods of a nature preserve provided an unbroken carpet of leafy boughs across the floor of the small valley. It was a beautiful view, and it was easy for Shelly to understand why they had chosen this spot.

Shelly suddenly frowned. A narrow gravel road circled the cemetery's perimeter, including the near edge of the ravine. A hundred yards away and to the left she noticed a lone car, a dark sedan, parked just off the road in the shadows beneath an oak. A man stood next to the tree's trunk in a long dark coat. At this distance it was hard to tell, but he seemed abnormally large, well over six feet with the broad shoulders of a football player. And he seemed to be watching Shelly.

A touch on her shoulder made Shelly jump in surprise. She turned and found a thirtyish man an inch or so taller than her, with dark hair slicked back and a thin white scar above his left eye. John Lane was one of the few people who didn't look out of place dressed in black, Shelly thought. He was one of her father's part-time operatives, a licensed private investigator R. Sherlock could call on when he needed another pair of hands on a case or when his case-load got too heavy. John was the one R. Sherlock most trusted, Shelly knew, and he was her favorite. When she was younger he was always doing little magic tricks to amuse her, and he was a terrific storyteller. In fact, when he wasn't working for her father, he wrote mystery novels and stories to help support himself.

"Hi, John," Shelly said. "Pretty crummy day for a funeral, huh?"

"I don't know that there's such a thing as a good day for a funeral, kiddo. How're you hold-ing up?"

Shelly suddenly remembered the large man by the oak, but when she looked back, the car was pulling away. He was probably just someone who came for the funeral and wanted to avoid the crowd, she thought. "Okay, I guess," Shelly said. "You?"

"Me?" He snorted a laugh. "You've got enough on your plate, kiddo, don't be worrying about me. I'll miss your mom and dad a lot more than the income. I've always got my stories to fall back on."

"Don't go falling where I can't find you," Shelly said, giving him a meaningful look. "The Holmes Investigative Agency may still need you."

"Is that so?" he mused. "How do you figure?"

Shelly shrugged. "I'm still thinking things over. If I find a way to keep the office open, I'm going to need a licensed investigator to handle cases."

"Because you're an unlicensed seventeen-year-old girl," he said nodding. "You know, kiddo, most people aren't going to buy that, even if you do have agents like me handling cases while you just manage."

"I *am* a Holmes," Shelly said.

"You sure are," John agreed, "and you've got your father's gifts, I know that. But the rest of the world doesn't. They're going to see a sweet little girl and draw their own conclusions. When someone's been robbed or kidnapped, you want to hire someone you feel can do the job." John shrugged. "I'm not trying to talk you out of it, Shelly, but you should know what kind of problems you'll be facing."

She nodded thoughtfully. Up until now she had been thinking her biggest problem would be getting her idea past Kevin and Uncle Joe.

"I'll think about it, John, thanks," she said, and gave him a hug.

"No charge, kiddo. Hang in there."

Shelly walked back toward the parking area as if in a daze. John was right. People only hired a private investigator when they faced desperate, critical problems. If there was any sort of doubt about an agency's ability to deal with such problems, they would go somewhere else, somewhere they would feel more confident and secure. Shelly had to admit, she would be dubious about going to an agency headed by a newly graduated high school student, but she was no ordinary teenager. She had a sharp mind and the benefit of her father's training and advice. She could do a good job as head of the agency. She just needed to convince the rest of the world.

How could she do this? The answer came immediately. She needed to solve some sort of case to prove that she was a good investigator. The Back Bay Slayer case was the only pending case she knew of at the agency. She realized it wasn't very realistic to think she might be able to crack a case that had stumped the entire city police department as well as her father, but if she could, it would give her all of the credibility and publicity she could hope for.

The police would not accept her working on the case, and investigating in the field would be next to impossible without their cooperation, not to mention dangerous. She made a deal with herself. She would read through her father's files on the case and see what she could come up with. Perhaps Julie and her expertise on serial killers could shed some light on some aspect of the case that had eluded the police. It was worth a try, she decided.

She saw Mrs. Dunn standing alone by her car, waiting for her husband. She had been crying, but Shelly saw her try to look strong when she noticed Shelly approaching. Shelly hugged her.

"Shelly, dear, how are you?" Mrs. Dunn asked with abundant concern.

"I'm okay," Shelly said. "And you?"

"It's just such a shock."

"I know." She paused a moment, deciding how to approach this. She knew Mrs. Dunn would be resistant to Shelly looking into the Back Bay Slayer case, so she had to be careful. "Mrs. Dunn, I know tomorrow is Memorial Day, but is there any way I can get into the office?"

"If you like, certainly," Mrs. Dunn said. "May I ask why?"

"I want to look through some of my father's things," Shelly said. It wasn't a lie, though it was extremely vague.

Mrs. Dunn didn't press her. "Would you like me to pick you up in the morning?"

"No, thanks," Shelly said. "I have my mom's car. How's 9:00 A.M.?"

"That would be fine. But are you sure you wouldn't rather wait a bit? Perhaps next week would be better."

"No. I'd rather do it sooner than later."

"That's exactly what your father used to say," Mrs. Dunn said, misting up. Shelly hugged her again and then said good-bye.

Shelly started to look for Kevin, to say good-bye to him as well. Uncle Joe would be taking him to the airport shortly. He would be back early Tuesday for the reading of the will, but Shelly didn't want to miss this chance to see him.

She ran into Toby first, who was there with his parents.

"Hi, Shelly," he said. "My mom wanted me to offer—well, so did I but it was her idea—to have you come along with us tomorrow. We're going to have a picnic, us and a few other families from our neighborhood. She thought maybe you wouldn't want to be alone."

"That's really sweet of both of you," Shelly said, "but I just made arrangements to spend the day at my father's office, sorting through some stuff. I really need to take care of it."

"No problem, I understand," he said. "If

you're going to be there all day, maybe I'll drop by after the picnic."

"Sure," Shelly said, "I could show you around. My dad was a really cool guy" Then she spotted Kevin by Uncle Joe's car. "I've got to go. Say thanks to your mom for me. And maybe I'll see you tomorrow."

When Shelly turned to go over to Kevin, she saw the dark sedan that had been parked beneath the oak. It was a black Ford with tinted windows, and it was driving through the parking area not thirty feet away. It had slowed near her, but as she looked at its tinted windows, it drove swiftly away.

Shelly woke to an empty house the next morning. Getting ready to face the day without her father complaining about how much time she spent in the bathroom or her mother urging her to eat a balanced breakfast seemed odd, but Shelly tried not to think about it. Instead, she focused on her plans for the day, her plans for the agency's future.

The clouds from the day before had broken and the sun was back, so Shelly decided to ride her bike to the office. She rolled down the ramp into the underground parking garage and found it empty except for a few cars parked by the elevator. Everyone was off for the holiday. One of the car's was Mrs. Dunn's Toyota, Shelly noted.

She locked up her bike and took the elevator up to the main floor to pass through security.

She knew the uniformed man whose round face looked up from a newspaper when the elevator doors opened. "Hi, Harry," she said as she reached the security desk.

"Morning, Miss Holmes. Sorry to hear about your mom and dad."

"Thanks. Pretty quiet today, huh?"

"I'm not complaining," Harry answered. He held up the paper to show Shelly the crossword puzzle he was working on. "I could get used to this. Say, you wouldn't happen to know an eight-letter word for 'Greek boulder-roller,' would you?"

Shelly smiled, recalling the research she had done for her humanities essay last week. "Sisyphus," she said and spelled it for him. "In Greek mythology, he ticked off Zeus and was condemned to roll a boulder up a hill eternally. Whenever he reached the top, the boulder would escape him and roll back to the bottom of the hill."

"Hey, great!" Harry exclaimed, filling in the blank squares. "You sure must have inherited you father's mind."

"Thanks, Harry," she said as she passed the security desk and headed for the elevators. Now I just have to convince the rest of the world of that, she thought. She hoped it would prove easier than Sisyphus's task.

Shelly rode the elevator up to the agency's floor. Not all of the lights were on in the hallway, as no one else seemed to be on the floor. It was kind of scary and kind of exciting at the same time, like being locked in a store after-hours. But the doors to the Holmes Investigative Agency were unlocked, and the lights were on and welcoming. Mrs. Dunn sat behind her desk as usual.

"Hi, Mrs. Dunn," Shelly said. "Sorry to bring you in on a holiday like this, but thanks."

"That's okay, Shelly," she said. "Besides, it's a good thing I was here. The police came a little while ago to collect some of your father's files."

"On the Back Bay Slayer?" Shelly said, not thinking to conceal her distress.

"Why, yes," Mrs. Dunn replied. "I'm surprised your father told you about that nasty business. The police came by with a warrant to recover all of the classified information in his possession, considering that he's no longer able to pursue the case. Why are you so upset?"

Shelly sighed and then confessed her plan to solve the case and gain enough credibility to keep the office open. Mrs. Dunn was understanding in a parental sort of way.

"I think your father would have been proud of your determination to try to keep the agency open," she said.

"I'm not giving up," Shelly told her. "Even if we don't make any money, I should inherit enough to keep the agency going for years. Uncle Joe will have a fit, but it's my money, and I can do whatever I want to with it. I just hope you're willing to stay while why I figure things out. I'm sure I couldn't run this place without you."

Mrs. Dunn smiled. "Of course I will." Then she sat up straight and said, "What can I do to help, boss?"

Shelly managed a small laugh, but her plans had been mostly deflated by the police taking those files. She wasn't sure what to do now. "I guess I'm just going to look through the box of stuff from Grandpa Emmet. I'm going to have to come up with a new plan, I guess. There's really no reason for you to stay any longer, if you'll show me how to set the alarm and lock up when I'm finished."

"If you're sure," Mrs. Dunn said. "I already changed the answering machine message to let people know we're closed until further notice. Other than that, I can't think of anything that I can do today, with everything closed for the holiday. And Sidney's at home, and I would like to spend some time with him. Okay, take this notepad and I'll walk you through the alarm system."

Shelly took the pad and took notes while Mrs.

Dunn instructed her on the operation of the alarm system. It really wasn't very complicated, and Shelly didn't think she would have to consult her notes, but she was glad to have them anyway in case she forgot a step. Then Mrs. Dunn collected her things and bid her good day.

Shelly locked the door behind Mrs. Dunn and then went into her father's office, swinging the door all the way open to draw out the squealing of the unoiled hinges. She started to go to the safe, but then her father's voice spoke in her head, telling her that leaving the doors open while she opened the safe was not good security, even when the building was empty. Shelly closed the doors and then opened the safe.

She opened the cardboard box from Grandpa Emmet and pulled out the photographs. Then she came to the manila envelope packed with letters to Sherlock Holmes. She poured them out on the carpet and sat in their midst, reading them one by one.

She found them fascinating, describing mysterious disappearances and baffling crimes that had taken place around the world. Shelly savored each like candy, but found them frustrating at the same time. Here were dozens of cases she could solve to impress the world, but they involved locations hundreds and thousands of miles away and people who had been dead for decades. The letters might offer up good ideas for John Lane's mystery stories, but they didn't seem to hold much promise for launching Shelly's investigative career. Still, they were too intriguing to stop reading. One after another, into the afternoon, Shelly read the letters. And around 2:00 she found the one that offered her new hope in her fight to keep the agency going.

Chapter Thirteen

The letter read:

Dear Mr. Holmes:

I read in the paper of your retirement to New York. I am a neighbor to the north, in Boston, and I implore you to consider taking on one more case. I desperately need your help. Only a man of your remarkable intellect can help me.

I was duped into entering into a land deal with a man I thought my friend, Charles Lapidis. He double-crossed me and cheated me of my land, fortune, and dignity. Everyone who could support my story has been paid off or worse. Two individuals involved have died under suspicious circumstances!

I beg for your help, not for my sake, but for that of my son, Michael. I used every cent I had to buy that land for his future, and now I have nothing to leave him.

I anxiously await your response.

Yours truly,

R. J. Tambler

Tambler. The name seemed familiar, and after a second Shelly placed it. There was a local TV news reporter named Jackie Tambler who was from this area. Shelly ran out to Mrs. Dunn's desk and checked the phone book. There were no Tamblers listed. Being a TV personality, it was reasonable to expect she would have an unlisted number, but it was the absence of any others that encouraged Shelly. Tambler was not a common name, and lack of any other Tamblers made it seem that much more likely that Jackie Tambler might be a descendant of the writer of the letter.

Excited that she might have found a case, even a seventy-year-old one, that she might be able to solve, Shelly packed the rest of the letters and photos back in the box and returned it to the safe. With R. J. Tambler's letter in her pocket, Shelly returned to the outer office and prepared to close up. She flipped off the lights and then went over to the keypad next to the doors to set the alarm. She stopped before she punched any buttons and realized that before she proceeded, she should try calling Jackie Tambler at the TV station to see if she was related to R. J. Tambler and if she could give Shelly any information. Shelly went back to Mrs. Dunns' desk and flipped on her desk lamp.

As she was pulling the phone book out again, she heard the *ping* of the elevator opening down

the hall. With all of the other offices on the
floor closed, Shelly couldn't imagine why anyone
else would be up here. She realized how alone
she was, and she switched off the desk lamp, the
only light, casting the room in darkness. Some
light came in from the hallway, but the corner in
which Shelly tensely waited behind Mrs. Dunn's
desk was shrouded in darkness.

A few seconds later a silhouette slipped in
front of the door, the vague shape of a man in a
hat. Shelly's breath caught in her throat as the
silhouette remained in front of the door. At first
she thought she was mistaken, but as she continued to stare her initial impression was confirmed: The man had only one arm.

There was a metallic rattling sound, only
barely audible through the glass doors. He's trying to get in, Shelly screamed in her head. She
eyed the control panel for the alarm, its green
light glowing brightly next to the doors. She
considered running over to it and triggering the
alarm, but if the man got in before help could
arrive...Shelly sank down behind the desk and
continued to watch the man, hoping he would
be unable to get the door open. A moment later
this hope proved to be futile as a decisive click
filled the silent office. The door swung open.

Shelly crouched further behind the desk. She
had a tremendous urge to scream and bit her fist
to keep herself from crying out. Who was this

man? He was too thin to be the man who was watching her at the funeral yesterday.

She heard a contemptuous snort from across the room. "The freaking alarm isn't even set," a hoarse voice muttered.

Shelly listened for the man's footsteps but heard nothing. She was about to peek around the corner of the desk to see if he was still in the room when a dark shape passed a few feet in front of her face. Shelly stopped breathing. The shape paused outside the doors to her father's office. The doorknob turned, and the door groaned like an obstinate nail being pulled from an old board.

"Good grief, Holmes, are you haunting the place already?" the hoarse voice said with a chuckle.

Then the shadow drifted into the inner office. Shelly thought now was the best time to make a break for it. She could dash across the room, trigger the alarm, and slip out the door in a few seconds. The one-armed man might not even notice her if she was quiet. Part of her was too scared to move. That part wanted her to stay right where she was, with her hands over her eyes, hoping the one-armed man would leave without discovering her. But what if he *did* find her? It wasn't something to think about.

Shelly quietly stood up behind the desk. There was no sound from within the inner office, but the door was still wide open. She took a deep breath and *moved*. She reached the doors and slapped at the control panel for the alarm. She only needed to flip a single switch to activate it. She groped for the switch, her nervous fingers pushing and pulling whatever they touched.

"Hey!" called a voice from the office. Raised as it was, the voice did not seem hoarse so much as a rough-edged roar.

Shelly's fingers continued to scramble blindly about the control panel, and finally she was rewarded by the green light going out and the red light going on. The alarm was set, with no time delay to allow anyone to leave the office. Shelly yanked the door open. The red light started blinking immediately. The alarm had been set off, and unless the intruder knew the four-digit access code, there was no way he could turn it off.

"Hold it!" the voice roared, sounding very close behind her.

Shelly charged through the door, afraid that if she looked back, she'd see the one-armed man right behind her, grasping her long hair in his single fist. She pelted down the hallway and passed the elevator. Even if it were waiting on this floor for someone to push the button and step in, it would still be too slow. The one-armed man would get there before the doors closed. Instead, she headed for the stairway, marked by a glowing red EXIT sign.

Shelly hit the dull gray fire door so it slammed back into the painted cinder-block wall with a crash that echoed ten stories up and down. She launched herself down the stairs, her hand gliding down the rail in case she tripped during her headlong descent down the stairway. The stairway took a right-angled turn every ten feet or so, and Shelly went around these corners at full speed, her arm clutching the rail and feeling the strain. She tried to listen as she ran, trying to hear pursuing footsteps over the pounding of blood in her ears and the racket of her own wild charge down the stairs. She couldn't hear anything else, but she didn't dare stop to listen, didn't dare even look back, until she reached the main floor and burst through another fire door out into the lobby.

The security desk was vacant. She stood there a moment, slightly dizzy from the winding stairs, her heart racing.

"Harry!" she called, as she jogged to the security desk. "Harry, where are you?"

The men's room was her first thought. The one in the lobby was only a few steps from the security desk. She pushed open the door. "Harry, are you in here?"

There was no answer, but behind her she heard the *ping* announcing the arrival of an elevator on this floor. She went all the way into the men's room and let the door close behind her. It could be Harry, she thought—or it could be the one-armed man. She hid in one of the stalls, standing on the toilet so her feet wouldn't show, and tried to figure out what to do next.

Harry would have seen the alarm go off on his security console, Shelly reasoned. He probably thought she had set it of accidentally and went upstairs to tell her. With a sudden chill deep inside her, she realized he would be completely off guard to face the one-armed man.

Then her worries turned back from Harry to herself. The ladies' room was on the other side of the wall behind Shelly, and through it she heard the door slam open. Then there was a series of crashes, like the stall doors being kicked open, one after another. She hoped desperately that he wouldn't search for her in the men's room—or that he didn't have to go to the bath-room!

Silence was restored second's later, but Shelly kept straining to hear anything else, any signs of the one-armed man's continued search. She kept waiting for the men's room door to crash open, for footsteps coming closer across the tile and stopping in front of her stall, and for the violent opening of its door a moment later.

But minutes passed, and nothing happened. No sounds at all came from the lobby. Shelly kept track on her watch, wondering how long she should wait until she was sure it was safe. She was hoping she would hear Harry return soon, and then she could...

The men's room door opened. Footsteps scuffed softly across the tile and stopped right outside the stall Shelly occupied. Beneath the door she saw a pair of high-topped sneakers. Someone tried the stall door and found it locked.

"Sorry," came a familiar voice, the last one she had expected to hear.

"Toby?" Shelly asked, scrambling to unlock the stall door.

"Shelly?" he responded with a mixture of surprise and confusion. "What are you doing in the men's room?"

"Boy am I glad to see you!" She hugged him and then pulled away to ask, "Was there anyone at the security desk when you passed by?"

"No. I figured they didn't have anyone on duty on a holiday. Why?"

"I'll explain later," she said. "Right now I need your help."

"Okay," he said, and then somewhat uncomfortably, "but, uh, could you give me a minute alone in here first?"

In spite of the tension, Shelly couldn't help smiling. "Sure."

Her watch told her it had been 15 minutes

since the one-armed man had searched the ladies' room. Shelly doubted he was still in the building. He would have assumed she got in contact with the police by now and escaped while he could. Still, when she went out into the stillness of the lobby, she hid herself behind the security desk, just in case.

When the men's room door opened a minute later, there came a *ping* from the elevators. Toby started to talk, but Shelly held up a hand to silence him until the elevator doors opened, revealing Harry holding a bleeding cut on his forehead.

"Harry!" Shelly exclaimed. "Should I call for an ambulance?"

Toby ran over to help him. "Are you okay, mister?"

"Someone hit me from behind," Harry grumbled. "Cut my head when I fell. Shoot, I thought you tripped the alarm by accident. Wasn't ready for anything like that."

"Come over here and sit down," Shelly said, leading him to the security desk.

"I'll get some paper towels," Toby said.

"Run some under cold water," Shelly told him as he dashed back to the men's room.

"I'll be okay," Harry said. Shelly could tell his professional pride had suffered more injury than his head. Once Toby came back with the cool, damp towels, they got the bleeding stopped and he seemed fine.

"Did you get a look at him?" Harry asked.

"Only in shadows. All I can say is he's a white male, skinny, about six feet tall, and he only has one arm."

Toby gave her a strange look and mouthed, "One arm?"

Harry said, "I need to call this in to my boss and notify the police."

"Okay," Shelly said. "We're going to go lock up the office."

"You kids be careful," Harry called after them.

"You think this one-armed guy might still be around?" Toby asked her.

"No way. Guys like him make sure to be far away by the time the police arrive."

They got into the elevator, and Shelly pushed the button for the tenth floor. "What are you doing here?" she asked.

Toby shrugged. "You offered me a tour yesterday, remember?"

"Oh, yeah," Shelly said. She had forgotten. "I guess now's as good a time as any."

Shelly showed him around the office, at the same time checking to see if she could tell what the one-armed man had been looking for. If he had searched the office, he was very good, she concluded. She couldn't even tell that he had been here. Then she and Toby reset the alarm and locked up.

Back in the lobby, the police had arrived, and Shelly told them what she had seen. Harry was back to his usual self, with just a small band-aid on his forehead to indicate that anything amiss had taken place.

Shelly and Toby took the elevator down to the parking garage. "I left my bike chained up outside the side door," Toby said.

"Mine's in the garage," Shelly said.

"I know. I saw it."

"We'll get mine first and then go get yours."

When they reached the parking level, the doors opened and they stepped out. Right away, Shelly saw there was something wrong with her bike. The tires were slashed.

"Terrific," she said.

At the far end of the parking garage, an engine started, amazingly loud in the enclosed garage. Shelly saw a black sedan pull out of a parking space and head right toward them.

"Come on!" she called, sprinting for the side door.

"I'm with you," Toby said, right behind her.

The car swerved to keep them in the bright circles of its headlights. Shelly couldn't stand to look into the blinding lights, but from the first glimpse she had gotten she was sure it was the same car that had been at the funeral yesterday.

Shelly and Toby reached the side door, and she kicked the wooden wedge holding it open out of place as she went through. The door swung closed and clicked as it locked behind them, sealing off the angry roar of the engine in the parking garage.

Toby swiftly unlocked his bike. "Hop on," he said, and seconds later they were breezing down the sidewalk on their way to Shelly's house.

"I didn't realize the detective business was so dangerous, Shelly," Toby said over his shoulder.

"I guess I didn't either." Or so exciting, she thought.

Chapter Fourteen

Shelly was so absorbed in thoughts of the one-armed man and R. J. Tambler's letter that it was only when they reached her neighborhood that she began to realize how much she liked having her arms around Toby. He had pedaled most of the way without a word, but just having him there in front of her was a comfort. As they rolled up her driveway, she was sorry the ride was ending.

When Toby came to a stop, she climbed off and circled around to face him. "Thanks for the ride," she said, smiling gratefully.

He smiled back. "Any time. I'm really glad I went to see you. But what about your bike?"

"I'll pick it up tomorrow, when there'll be more people around. I'll call you if I need a bodyguard."

Toby said, "Call me even if you don't."

Shelly nodded. "Tonight."

"You better," he said as he let his bike roll back down the driveway, "or I'll have to come looking for you again."

Shelly waved as he rode off, and then she went inside to start acting on the plans she had made during the ride home. There wasn't much she could do about the one-armed man at this point except hope that the police caught him, so she decided to focus on R. J. Tambler's letter.

She had several ideas on how to proceed. She could go to the library and research the Lapidis and Tambler families, but it would be closed, this being Memorial Day. Her friend Nick, who owned Baker Street Books, was something of an expert on local history and might be of help, but the book shop would be closed today also. So Shelly decided to start with Jackie Tambler, the TV reporter. The news never takes a holiday, Shelly knew, so Jackie would probably be working. Shelly found the number of the TV station in the phone book and dialed it.

Using the phone made her remember her promise to call Toby tonight, and she was already looking forward to it. An operator answered, and Shelly asked to be connected with Jackie Tambler. She was surprised when the operator put her call right through, but Shelly's flush of success was short-lived. A prim-voiced woman answered, "Jackie Tambler's office."

"Ms. Tambler, please," Shelly said, trying to sound important.

"Who may I say is calling?" the voice asked with a machine-like lack of feeling.

"Shelly Holmes."

"One moment, please."

Ice skating rink music filled Shelly's ear, and she looked dejectedly at the phone in her hand.

A busy woman like Jackie Tambler wouldn't talk to just anyone who called. Shelly was going to have to find some sneaky way—

"Hello?" said a new voice, one Shelly recognized from TV. "This is Jackie Tambler."

Shelly excitedly returned the phone to her ear. "Ms. Tambler! Hello. My name is Shelly Holmes."

"Daughter of R. Sherlock and Mary Holmes." Jackie's voice was so familiar from hearing it on the news, it was like talking to an old friend. "Yes, Shelly, I know who you are. I'm terribly sorry about your parents. How are you doing?"

"Okay, I guess. I know you're a busy woman, so I'll try to be quick. I've been going through some old papers, and I happened across a letter that a Mr. R. J. Tambler wrote to my great-grandfather."

"Really?" Jackie sounded genuinely interested. "R. J. Tambler was *my* great-grandfather. It must have had to do with the property that was swindled away from him."

"Exactly," Shelly said. "I'd like to ask you a few questions about it."

"Hm," Jackie said thoughtfully. "Why are you so interested in this? That happened over 70 years ago."

"Curiosity," Shelly said. "It runs in my family."

"So I've heard. Are you thinking of following

in your father's footsteps?"

"Well…"

"Maybe we can work out a little deal," Jackie said.

The mention of deals made Shelly wary. "What kind of deal?"

"I'll answer your questions, if you'll answer mine…on television. I think you'd make a great interview subject."

The thought sent butterflies winging around in Shelly's stomach.

"I don't know…"

"I'll tell you what," Jackie said. "Let's meet for lunch. Say, at Riley's in an hour? I'll tell you what I know about R. J.'s land deal, and you can give me your answer about the interview. No pressure."

"That sounds very nice," Shelly said. "I'll see you in an hour."

Shelly figured it would take her about half an hour to get downtown to Riley's. This left her with thirty minutes, most of which she spent trying to figure out which outfit to wear. The thought of having lunch with Jackie Tambler made her feel like her stomach had been pumped full of helium. The woman was so strong and successful, everything Shelly hoped to be someday in her own field. She finally opted for a simple skirt and blouse combination and the pendant her parents had given her as a graduation present.

She wondered what her parents would have thought of her decision to take over the agency. She was sure her father would have been proud. Her mother would have worried about the danger, of course, but Shelly thought she would understand and that she would be proud, too.

When she slipped into the driver's seat of her mother's Lincoln, Shelly found the sunglasses she had given her mother for her birthday last year, and she almost started to cry. Instead, she took a deep breath and moved the sunglasses to the passenger seat. She thought of her mom riding next her when she was learning how to drive, watching over her, ready with a quick warning or a bit of advice or word of praise. As she drove to her lunch meeting, Shelly hoped that her mother, wherever she was, was still watching over her.

At Riley's, Shelly told the hostess she was there to meet Jackie Tambler.

"Oh, yes, Ms. Tambler's already arrived."

The hostess guided Shelly across the expanse of forest-green carpeting that filled the paneled dining room to a table for two near the back, where tall windows afforded a view of the Charles River. Shelly thanked the hostess and then approached Jackie Tambler.

She looked much as she did on television, with artfully styled auburn hair and the most friendly smile Shelly had ever encountered. She stood to greet Shelly.

"Shelly, hi, it's nice to meet you," she said, gesturing for Shelly to take the chair opposite hers.

"I really want to thank you, Ms. Tambler…"

"Call me, Jackie, please."

"Okay. Anyway, I'm very grateful that you're taking the time to talk to me."

Jackie said, "Are you kidding? Even if you decide against the interview, you're doing me a favor. R. J.—everyone called my great-grandfather R. J.—was a very sweet man, if a little naive about business. He passed away when I was a little girl, but I heard all of the stories about how Charles Lapidis swindled him. Hardly anyone believed R. J., but he was too good a man to make up such a story. I don't care much about the land, but it would mean a lot to me if you could prove he was telling the truth."

A red-headed waitress in a green and white outfit stopped at their table to take their orders. Shelly flipped open the menu in front of her and ordered the first thing that caught her eye, a turkey club sandwich. Jackie ordered a chef salad, and then the waitress bustled off toward the kitchen.

"So where do you want to start?" Jackie asked.

Shelly pulled her notebook from her purse and readied a pen. "How about with everything you know about the deal between your great-grandfather and Charles Lapidis."

Jackie nodded and leaned back in her chair, her eyes wandering upward as she searched her memory. "R. J. was a sailor, working on cargo ships sailing around the world. He managed to save up a good bit of money, and after he married my great-grandmother and had a son, he decided he should give up sailing so he could be with his family. He got a job in the shipyards that would support them, and then he started looking for a way to invest the money he'd saved so one day he could pass it on to his son."

Jackie paused when the waitress brought them glasses of water and then continued. "Charles Lapidis had a good reputation in his business dealings and a knack for making lucrative real estate deals. R. J. met him through a friend and mentioned his desire to find an investment. Mr. Lapidis came to him several weeks later with a proposition. A man with quite a bit of land near Hyannis was looking to sell off a significant amount of his holdings, keeping only the small lot with his home on it. Real estate in that area looked like a good bet, but there were two problems. First, the owner wanted twice what my grandfather could afford, and second, he was picky about his neighbors and would not sell to a sailor."

Jackie stopped and took a sip of her water. Shelly admired how clearly and compellingly she told the story. It was easy to see how she had risen so high in her profession.

"Mr. Lapidis proposed that he purchase the land in his name alone and then sell a half share to R. J. My great grandfather agreed and hired an attorney to represent him in the deal. Mr. Lapidis bought the property and then met secretly with R. J. and his attorney. The new title was drawn up, and R. J.'s lawyer went to file it with the city. But the lawyer never reached the courthouse. R. J. heard of the murder the next day and went to see Mr. Lapidis, who claimed he knew nothing of any deal with him. Mr. Lapidis's lawyer denied ever meeting R. J. There was a bank record that R. J. had withdrawn the money, but the only documents recording who it had been paid to were stolen from his attorney. The owner of the roadside inn where R. J. and Mr. Lapidis had struck their deal mysteriously came into a good deal of money and moved to New York. A farmer who saw them at the inn together disappeared with no explanation. R. J. suspected that Mr. Lapidis had him killed, just like the attorney."

The air of dread that lingered after Jackie finished was dissipated by the arrival of the waitress with their lunch. As Shelly absently picked up a french fry, she said, "That's quite a story."

Jackie nodded and speared a wedge of tomato with her fork. "Charles Lapidis was a slick one.

People still think he was an upright business man." She waved the fork and piece of tomato in Shelly's direction. "As far as I can see, there's only one way you can prove Lapidis was a swindler. After seventy years, it's going to be pretty tough, but there is one chance."

Shelly raised her eyebrows expectantly.

"R. J. talked with Mr. Lapidis a number of times over the years after the swindle. Charles Lapidis wasn't just a crook. He had a genuine cruel streak. He told R. J. that he still had the land title that listed R. J. Tambler as half-owner. He liked to tease R. J. that maybe he would send it to him some day—or maybe he would burn it instead. R. J. thought Mr. Lapidis was trying to tempt him into breaking into his house, so Mr. Lapidis could have him arrested. My great-grandfather never fell for it—he said if a dog bit you once it was the dog's fault, but if it bit you twice, it was your fault—but he was sure Mr. Lapidis really did keep the title around. If you can find it, that will prove the whole thing once and for all."

Shelly took a bite of her sandwich and chewed thoughtfully. Jackie was right—all she had to do was find a piece of paper hidden by a very shrewd criminal over 70 years ago. A slim chance, but better than no chance.

"About the interview," Shelly said. Jackie looked up from her salad expectantly. "I'll do it, but could we wait a week or so? Maybe if I solve this case we'd have something interesting to talk about." And then I can announce I'm going to keep the agency open, she thought.

Jackie gave her a warm smile. "I'm sure you're interesting enough for a dozen interviews, but you're right. That would make a good story. And I am kind of busy at the moment anyway, covering the harbor murders. Next week sounds good."

An electronic chirping started coming from Jackie's purse, and she pulled out a beeper. She looked at it and then looked apologetically at Shelly. "Speaking of busy…"

"I understand," Shelly said. "I'll let you know how it goes."

Jackie slid a business card across the table. "Do that. My home number's on there as well as my direct line at the office. Call any time." She stood and made ready to leave. "I'll take care of the bill on the way out. Take your time and enjoy lunch."

"Thanks," Shelly called after her.

After Jackie had left the restaurant, Shelly returned to her sandwich, and to her thoughts. She really liked Jackie, which gave her yet another reason to want to solve this crime. She didn't think she could wait until tomorrow for the library and Baker Street Books to open. She thought she had Nick's home phone number in her room and decided to go back to the house to look for it. Perhaps he would be able to tell her more about Lapidis.

Shelly played the radio on the way home, but as anxious as she was to make progress on this case the drive seemed to take forever. She left the Lincoln in the driveway and hurried to the front door. Her key clicked in the lock, and the door swung open. So intent was she on her thoughts that she had the door closed and was starting to walk across the room before she noticed that it had been trashed.

The paintings had been torn off the walls and slashed. The furniture was flipped over and cushions shredded. Books had been pulled from their shelves. She could see through the door into her father's den that it was an even bigger mess.

Shelly got her shock under control and tried to figure out what to do. The vague, threatening image of the one-armed man flashed through her mind, and she realized that whoever had done this might still be here. She turned to rush back out the front door to call the police from her neighbor's house, but as she did so she glanced out the front window and saw a dark sedan pull into the driveway behind the Lincoln.

Chapter Fifteen

The door of the sedan opened and a monstrously large hand came out and gripped the door. The huge man she had seen watching her at the funeral emerged from the car and glanced up the street at the other houses. There was no one in sight. He started up the front walk.

Shelly fled. She wasn't sure if the hulking man was working on his own or with the one-armed man, but she didn't want to find out in a one-on-one confrontation with no witnesses. She ran through the house to her mother's sculpting studio and slid open the glass door that let out into the back yard. She sprinted through the garden to the back fence, thinking wildly that after all of this running from scary men she wasn't going to have to go jogging for a week. She scrambled over the fence into the Gorman's yard on the other side. Then she ran around their house, out onto Danson Street.

She hurried down the street wondering what to do next. She scolded herself for not getting the sedan's license number, but she wasn't about to go back to look. Her instinct was to go someplace where she would feel safe and then think about what to do next. The safest place she could think of was Julie's apartment. Her bike was still at the office, and the Lincoln was blocked in the driveway by the huge man's sedan. That left the bus, but that was okay because there was a stop not far away.

She turned onto Mason Street and at the corner a block away she saw a line of people boarding the bus. The next one wouldn't be by for fifteen or twenty minutes, and she didn't want to be waiting on the corner that long, in case the dark sedan should come prowling by. Shelly broke into a run. Halfway there, the line of passengers had finished boarding, and the doors closed with a hiss.

"Wait!" Shelly called, waving her arms, even though she knew she'd never be heard.

But the bus didn't pull away from the curb. A second later the doors opened again, and she saw the driver watching her, tapping his fingers on the steering wheel. With a feeling of tremendous relief, Shelly got out her bus pass and showed the driver, who nodded and closed the doors again.

"Thanks."

She sank into a seat, closed her eyes, and took a few deep breaths. Everything would be okay now. When she opened her eyes again, the bus was stopping at the intersection with the road she lived on. Practically right outside her window, waiting for the light to change, was the dark sedan. Shelly hunched down in her seat.

She peeked up to see if she could see the sedan's license number, but it was too close to the car in front of it.

The bus started moving again and drove through the intersection. She stood and looked out the back of the bus to see if the sedan followed, but when the light changed, it went straight. Shelly dropped back into her seat and waited to reach Julie's neighborhood.

Shelly called the police from Julie's apartment. Both Julie and Gail were there, and Spike, of course, and they went with her back to the house to meet the police. The huge man and his black sedan were nowhere in sight. The police looked around, but could find no obvious evidence of whoever had broken into the house. Shelly looked around but as far as she could tell there was nothing missing, only overturned and broken.

The police left after taking her statement and said they would let her know of any developments. Julie gave them her number and said Shelly could be reached there. She looked back at Shelly. "Is that all right with you?"

Shelly nodded. After the scare she'd had this afternoon and the ample evidence that the house was not secure, she did not think she'd be able to sleep here tonight.

Julie and Gail helped her straighten up the

house, and then she packed a bag with enough clothes to last her for a few days. She did remember to bring along her address book, and that night, after a relaxing dinner at a local Mexican place with Gail and Julie, she called Nick Cramer at home.

"Hi, Nick," she said when he answered. "This is Shelly Holmes."

"Well, Shelly, this is a surprise!" he said. Shelly thought Nick was around seventy, but he was one of the most energetic people she knew. He ran Baker Street Books all by himself and had done so for over thirty years. "I didn't get a chance to speak to you at the funeral, but you have my sympathy. The world is a lonelier place without your parents."

"Thanks, Nick. I was wondering if you could help me. Do you know anything about the Lapidis family?"

"Lapidis? Sure, I've heard of them. Nothing much lately. Old Charles has been dead, oh, forty years or so. Charles Jr. just passed away a few months back. Charles the third is doing time for insider trading or stock manipulation, one of those high-finance no-nos."

"Huh. Sounds like dirty tricks are a family tradition."

"Well, I don't know about that," Nick said. "I never heard tell of any such from Old Charles or Junior. Of course, maybe they just didn't get caught with both hands in the cookie jar like Charles III. What's all of this about, Shelly?"

Shelly knew she could trust Nick without reservation. He had been a friend of the family since before Shelly had been born. He had a mystery fan's interest in Sherlock Holmes—as demonstrated by the name of his shop—and he had met R. Sherlock when he first opened the agency. Nick loved to talk shop with her father, and her father had a voracious appetite for books so their relationship had flourished over the years. Knowing how much Nick loved a good mystery, Shelly couldn't hold out on him. She gave him all of the details.

"I see," he said when she was finished. "I tell you what I'll do, Shelly. I may have an acquaintance or two who had business dealings with the Lapidises. I'll do some calling around in the morning, and I'll see what I can find out for you."

"That'd be great, Nick," Shelly said. "Thanks."

Nick laughed. "Don't thank me yet. I haven't done anything. I'll let you know tomorrow if I find out anything."

"Okay. Good night, Nick."

"To you, too, Shelly."

The next morning Shelly drove to her aunt and uncle's home and rode with them to the legal offices of Baker & Friedman. Stephen Baker greeted them personally and led them to a meeting room with a long wooden table and a TV/VCR set-up in the corner. Coffee and donuts were laid out on a counter at the back of the room, but Shelly's aunt had made breakfast for everyone this morning. Shelly had eaten more out of a desire to make her aunt feel better than actual appetite and now was not the least bit hungry.

Shelly rolled one of the deep, plush chairs away from the table and sat across from her aunt and uncle. Kevin was supposed to have gotten into the airport a short time ago and taken a cab directly here, but he had yet to arrive. Stephen Baker was a handsome gray-haired man with a neat Van Dyke beard and a habit of scowling for no discernible reason. Shelly had met him a few times over the years but did not know him well. He encouraged everyone to partake of coffee and donuts, though he himself did not. He paced at the front of the room, occasionally taking a silver pocket watch on a chain from his waistcoat pocket to scowl at it briefly before putting it back and resuming his pacing.

Shelly spent the time lost in thoughts of her own. This morning she had thought to call her friends to let them know she was staying at Julie and Gail's. When Toby had heard why, he seemed angry with himself, that if he had stuck around instead of just dropping Shelly off and abandoning her yesterday afternoon, he could have protected her from the man in the dark sedan. Shelly did not say so, but even as athletic as Toby was, she didn't think Toby would have been able to stop the hulking man she had seen get out of that car. Still, when he insisted she promise to call him instead of going out alone, she did so. She told him about going to the library this afternoon, and he had immediately offered to go with her. She could think of worse ways to spend an afternoon.

Kevin finally showed up, led by a secretary who had shown him the way to the meeting room. He breezed in, apologizing for his tardiness, and kissed Shelly on top of her head. He sat next to her, said good morning to his aunt and uncle, and then looked expectantly at Stephen Baker.

"We're ready," the attorney said. "Good. We'll begin with the videotape." He picked up the remote control and continued speaking absently as he pressed buttons. "As it happens, Mary wanted to revise the will to specify that certain pieces of her artwork would go to the Chicago Art Institute, where she studied sculpting. While we were at it, we completely updated the will, and R. Sherlock and Mary had this videotape made."

The TV screen filled with a solid blackness

that lasted several seconds. Everyone in the room watched it expectantly, and then after a staticky break the image of R. Sherlock and Mary sitting on a sofa in an office appeared. An office in this building, Shelly guessed.

They looked at each other and laughed nervously. "Forgive me," R. Sherlock said in the resonant voice Shelly missed so much. She closed her eyes and fought back the tears. "I suppose if you're watching this it's not a light-hearted occasion. We're making this tape to explain some of the changes we've just made to our will. The document itself contains all of the legal details, but not the reasons and the feelings behind them. Except for Mary's sculptures, for which she's made special arrangements, our estate will be divided between our two children, Kevin and Shelly, though not quite evenly."

Kevin and Shelly exchanged a look, and she realized that seeing their parents talking and smiling and alive was as painful for him as it was to her.

"This was a decision that we felt we had to make," Mary Holmes said. "Kevin, Shelly, we love both of you very, very much, and equally. We want to treat you equally in this matter as well, but we find we can't quite do that. Kevin, you've known the path you wanted to travel through life almost since you were born. We're both very proud of your success, and we're sure you'll continue to flourish in your chosen field. Shelly, too, has had that same kind of single-mindedness about the path she wants to travel, though I may have been slow to recognize and support her choice. It's the mother in me, and I hope you realized that. Kevin, you've achieved your independence, and there's not much we can do to help you in your life and endeavors. You will each receive half of the financial and material parts of our estate; but, we're leaving the agency to Shelly."

Shelly's mouth dropped wide open. Uncle Joe and Aunt Tricia were looking at her in open astonishment.

"As your mother said," R. Sherlock continued, "we don't wish to show any preference, but Shelly has demonstrated not only an aptitude but a passion for my profession—*our* profession—and we think she deserves this opportunity. Shelly, sweetheart, the agency is now yours, but we don't want you to look at it as an obligation. You are not bound by any family tradition to keep it going. You can sell the agency, close it down, turn it into a museum—whatever you want. Because it *is* your business now. Whatever you do, remember that your mother and I are proud of you."

"Yes," Mary said. "Prouder than you can imagine."

Their faces froze and then the screen went

blank again. Mr. Baker focused on the remote control to shut it down. Shelly turned to look at Kevin and was amazed to find him wearing a grin.

"You're not upset?" Shelly asked.

"Me?" Kevin said, chuckling. "I think it's great. I never had any interest in the agency, but you lived and breathed it. The only thing that surprises me is that Mom was a willing participant. The way she worried…"

"She probably didn't think it would happen so soon," Shelly pointed out.

Kevin's smile faded. "Yeah."

Mr. Baker cleared his voice. "There are a few more major issues to cover," he said. "Miss Holmes, as you are still under eighteen, the will stipulates that your aunt and uncle become your legal guardians."

Shelly nodded.

"Personal possessions will be divided between the two of you. The house is to be available to Miss Holmes until five years after she has graduated from college, at which point it will be sold and the proceeds split between the two of you. If it is mutually agreeable, the house may be sold before that time."

There were lots of other little details, so many that Shelly lost track. The part that fascinated her most was the R. Sherlock and Mary Holmes Endowment for the Arts that Mary had set up, to be funded by the sale of her remaining works, the ones already displayed in galleries, others exhibited elsewhere, and the many stored at the house. She liked that her mother would be remembered and both her name and her father's would live on while helping artists like her mother.

Finally the reading came to an end, and Mr. Baker left them alone. Kevin checked his watch and said, "I hate to rush in and out like this," he said, "but I can just make the noon flight back to the Big Apple and get to rehearsals." He hugged Shelly. "Take care. And I'm still sending you tickets for opening night."

"I can't wait," Shelly said.

Then he departed and Shelly was left alone with her aunt and uncle. An awkward silence ensued.

"Legal guardians," Shelly said, as if to see what it sounded like out loud.

"Yes, well, it's only for a few months," Uncle Joe said. "We'll try to be accommodating, Shelly, but until your birthday we're responsible for your well-being. I hope you understand that."

Shelly nodded, not liking the ominous sound of that.

"We want you to move in with us," Aunt Tricia said suddenly. "We realize you're a very independent girl, but we can't have you living in that house all alone. What if there was an emergency?"

"I'm not living in the house," Shelly said. "I'm living with Julie and Gail at the moment." She didn't even consider telling them what had prompted her to move out yesterday; that would have ended the discussion right there. "That house is too big for one person and being around Spike makes me feel loved. I haven't asked Julie and Gail about staying with them permanently, but I think they'd say yes. Would that be all right with you?"

Uncle Joe and Aunt Tricia looked at each other. Uncle Joe nodded slowly.

"I know," Shelly replied.

"Well, if you really want to live with Gail, I guess it's okay with us."

"As for the agency…" Uncle Joe began.

"I'm not selling," Shelly said.

He held his hands up. "You've made that clear," he said with a smile. "I just wanted to tell you that, as the agency's accountant, I can come up with some possible scenarios for you. For instance, if you want to mothball it while you attend college."

"Oh, I'm sorry for being so defensive," Shelly said. "I need to think about it some more, and talk things over with Mrs. Dunn and John Lane. I'm sure I'm going to need your expertise, Uncle Joe, and I appreciate it. Thanks."

Actually, Shelly had a pretty good idea exactly

what she was going to do with the agency, but she needed to buy herself a little time to iron out the details—like solving a crime that had taken place over 70 years ago.

Shelly rode home with her aunt and uncle and then drove the Lincoln directly to Toby's to pick him up for their trip to the library. He was shooting hoops in the driveway while he was waiting, and when he saw her he tossed the ball into the bushes and ran over to her car.

"Sorry I'm late," Shelly said.

"No problem," Toby said with a wave of his hand. "Just gave me more time to practice my Michael Jordan moves."

"You want to be like Mike, huh?"

"Just don't tell anyone here in Celtic City that I'm a Bulls fan. Have you had lunch yet? I got paid for mowing lawns this morning. My treat."

"That sounds wonderful," Shelly said.

They had sandwiches at a deli not far from the library and then walked the rest of the way. Shelly sifted through the bulky indexes for the *Boston Globe* and *Boston Herald* and compiled a list of every mention of the Lapidis family. Toby helped her by getting the appropriate spools of microfilm, and then the two of them spent the rest of the afternoon at the microfilm readers, zipping through hundreds of newspaper pages to find the Lapidis articles. The machines allowed you to insert a quarter in a slot and photocopy articles of interest on slippery gray paper.

Shelly skimmed through articles to see if they were worth copying. The pieces on Charles Jr. and Charles III were of little help. The oldest articles, which documented Charles Sr.'s business deals and his doings around town, were also disappointing. From the portrait the newspaper painted, he was a pillar of the community, a friend of businessmen, and an advisor to politicians. Articles about his personal life were sketchier and mainly limited to his activities in the Boston Bibliophile's Club.

"What's a bibliophile?" Toby asked.

"Someone who collects books," Shelly said. She pretended not to notice the impressed look he gave her.

Charles Sr.'s obituary was the most glowing article of all, practically nominating the man for sainthood. It did mention near the end that the bulk of the Lapidis estate, including Charles's library, had been bequeathed to Charles Jr. Shelly made a note to ask Nick if he knew anything about the Lapidis library. Then she gathered up the sheaf of slippery gray photocopies and helped Toby return the reels of microfilm.

She had not learned anything earth-shattering, she told herself on the way home, but she had thoroughly versed herself in the history and background of the people involved, which was important. She dropped Toby off at home and thanked him for his help, and then she drove to Julie's apartment.

When she walked in, Spike greeted her enthusiastically. "Shelly?" came Gail's voice from her room, which was dark except for the glow of her computer monitor.

"Yes?"

"Your friend Nick called awhile ago. He'd like you to call him back."

"Okay," Shelly said. This was perfect, as she'd wanted to ask him about what she'd learned today anyway. After he answered the phone and they'd exchanged greetings, she said, "I was looking through old newspaper articles this afternoon and read that Charles Lapidis was a book collector. Do you know anything about what happened to his library?"

"Funny that you should ask," Nick said. "As of an hour or so ago, it's boxed up in the back room of my shop."

Chapter Sixteen

Shelly couldn't believe her ears.

"What do you mean the Lapidis library is in your back room?" she asked Nick.

"Just that," he replied, sounding very self-satisfied. "I told you I'd check around about the family. While I was doing that, I found that the present Mrs. Lapidis is selling off family possessions to cover the costs of appealing her husband's case. Charles III inherited his grandfather's books when Charles Jr. past away this winter. I rang up Mrs. Lapidis and inquired about the books, and she was only too happy to get rid of them, at a very reasonable price, I must say."

"That's terrific," Shelly said. She checked her watch. It was almost seven. "I suppose you're closed for the day."

"That I am," Nick confirmed. "However, I thought I would stick around for a few hours and see what treasures those boxes hold. If you'd like to come over…"

"I'll be there in fifteen minutes."

She hung up and grabbed her purse. She hesitated, wondering if she should call Toby. She had promised to call him rather than go out alone, but she had taken up most of his day at the library. She didn't want to take advantage of a good thing. Then Spike lumbered into the kitchen and sat, watching her with a dopey look on his face. That gave her an idea. She wouldn't go alone—she'd take Spike.

"Gail," Shelly called, "I'm going out again, and Spike's going with me."

"You going running this late?" Gail called back, concerned. The clicking of her keyboard stopped.

Shelly smiled. It was like having a Jamaican baby-sitter, but she liked having someone caring about her. "No, driving. I'm going to Nick's bookshop. He's got some new books he wants to show me."

"Okay. When do you suppose you'll be home?"

Home. Shelly hadn't yet caught Gail and Julie together to ask them about her moving in permanently. It sounded like Gail thought she already had. "By nine, probably. I'll call if I'm going to be later."

"Okay. Have a good time."

Shelly took Spike down to the Lincoln and let him in the passenger door. He hopped up on the seat, facing forward, and looked at her expectantly. Spike loved to ride in the car.

Shelly made the quick drive to Baker Street Books and pulled around to the back of the block, which was all a large, tree-lined parking lot for shoppers patronizing the shops that lined the side of the block facing Wendt Street. The parking lot was mostly empty, as the shops were all closed by this time, so Shelly was able to park close to the back of the long building that housed the shops. Narrow rows of shrubbery contained by concrete curbing separated the aisles of the parking lot, and bright lights high atop steel poles provided plenty of light.

Shelly got out of the car and went around to let Spike out. The parking lot was separated from the back of the building by a double-lane throughway for deliveries, garbage trucks, and other such traffic. Shelly noticed a pair of head-lights swiftly approaching along it. The lights of the parking lot reflected off the car's tinted wind-shield and windows. It was the black sedan. It stopped abruptly between Shelly and the build-ing.

The door opened and one huge foot stepped out. "Hold it!" said the gruff voice of the car's massive driver.

Shelly opened the passenger door and said, "Spike!"

The German shepherd came barreling out of the car, growling like a mad grizzly bear. It was if he could sense Shelly's fear and was responding to the threat, protecting her. He charged the black sedan with his long, white fangs gleaming in the light.

The large man's eyes opened wide, and in a

panic he almost shut his foot in the car door. A second after it closed, Spike's forepaws hit the glass, and he started barking, his muzzle so close to the window he was steaming it up.

The engine of the sedan revved and it shot away along the back of the building. Spike slipped off and followed to the center of the road, still barking. Shelly went to him, to keep him from chasing the car and threw her arms around him. "Good boy!" she said as she hugged him. "Good boy!"

The two of them watched the sedan reach the corner and turn out of sight. Unlike the last time she had seen the black sedan, this time the driver had not left her scared and shaken. This time she and Spike shared the same feeling of triumph. This time she had gotten his license plate number.

"Come on, boy," she called, leading Spike through an open corridor lined with benches and planters to the front of the building. The CLOSED sign was in the door of Baker Street Books, but Shelly found the door unlocked. After they were inside, she turned the deadbolt herself.

"Shelly?" called a voice from further back in the store.

"Yeah, Nick, it's me." Spike was sniffing a stack of old paperbacks by the counter. She dragged him away toward the back of the store.

"Come on, hero."

The books in the front part of the store were organized by category and alphabetized, but they overflowed the shelves and had to be stacked on the floor or in front of other books. This gave the place a comfortably disordered look. Shelly led Spike through the dark and narrow aisles where she had spent many hours when she was growing up, looking for something new and interesting to read. At the back of the store, a curtain separated the store itself from what Nick called his inner sanctum.

He had an old rolltop desk and a gooseneck lamp where he did paperwork. On shelves above it were his treasures: First editions of Sir Arthur Conan Doyle's Sherlock Holmes books and a framed photograph of Holmes with Doyle and Dr. Watson that Shelly's father had given him. The walls were covered with movie posters, book announcements, and framed newspaper articles all featuring Sherlock Holmes. Other than a small refrigerator that hummed busily, the rest of the space was filled with books not nearly so ordered as even those displayed in front. These were recent acquisitions, not yet sorted and priced, stored in the cardboard boxes and paper bags he had gotten them in. The inner sanctum was usually pretty crowded because of all of the books, but tonight it was so cramped there was scarcely room to move. A blockade of identical boxes, each large enough to hold a good-sized TV set, had been erected in the middle of the floor and almost filled the room.

Shelly whistled as she stood with the curtain pulled back. Nick was watching her from his seat at his desk, the light from the lamp reflected on his round, wire-rimmed glasses, open delight on his face.

"How many of them are there?" she asked.

"Books or boxes? Eighteen boxes. I have no idea how many books."

"I hope you didn't buy these just to help me..." Shelly started to say, but he waved it off.

"I know I can get a little carried away when the game is afoot, but not this time," he said. That phrase—"The game is afoot"—was one her great-grandfather used to utter when he and Watson were deeply into a mystery and something exciting was beginning to happen. It was Nick's favorite line, and it never failed to give Shelly goose bumps. "Mrs. Lapidis just wanted to get rid of the books in one lot. I only picked through one box when I went to see them, but I should be able to make my money back from the first editions in that box alone. Lapidis had himself quite a collection. It's a book dealer's dream. Shall we start looking through them?"

"Just a minute," Shelly said. "I need to make a phone call." She filled Nick in on the black sedan and the encounter in the parking lot, and then she called Sergeant Garcia. She told him about the man following her and gave him the license number. He said he would call her back at the book store or Gail and Julie's when he had something.

Then Nick and Shelly started going through the books. For the most part they had been crammed into the boxes without regard for their well-being. "Whoever packed these never loved a book in his life," Nick commented darkly as he and Shelly rescued the books from the boxes. She glanced at the titles as she unpacked them, not sure what she was looking for. Nick made small noises of pleasure on discovering certain volumes, and that kept Shelly amused as they went through box after box. They had no place to put the books except back in the boxes, as there was no room to leave them all unpacked, but Nick returned them to the boxes with care and stored them so as not to risk damaging the old bindings.

The seventh box they looked in contained old papers as well as books. Most were private letters, though a few were business receipts and records. Shelly scrutinized these for something that would help her, but they dealt with other matters entirely, legitimate matters as far as she could tell.

Nick seemed puzzled as he pulled several oversized volumes from the box. He thumbed through them and his eyebrows rose in mild surprise. "Business ledgers," he said, handing them to Shelly. "Someone must have thrown anything that was bound with a cover into these boxes."

She examined them as well, the accounting records of a fish wholesaler, a tavern, and several other small businesses Lapidis was involved in. Shelly closed the last one, her enthusiasm not as strong as it had been earlier. She was beginning to feel despondent of finding any clues to Mr. Lapidis's wrongdoing when Nick pulled another volume from the box. This one, like the ledgers, had no title on its spine or its leather cover, but it was much smaller, a little bigger than a paperback novel. Nick flipped through it and then looked appraisingly at Shelly.

"Would you perhaps be interested in the diary of Charles Lapidis, Sr.?" he asked.

"Give me, give me, give me!" Shelly said, shooting up from her seat on an old fruit crate.

But before Shelly had a chance to study it, the phone rang. Nick answered it and handed it to her.

"Shelly? This is Sergeant Garcia. The big guy who's been following you around? We've got him in custody. I think maybe you ought to come down here and talk to him."

Shelly made Nick promise to call her if he found anything else as promising as the diary, and then she called Gail to let her know she'd be later than 9:00. When Shelly told her why, Gail said, "Good going, girl! You tell that policeman friend of yours to lock this giant man up and throw away the key."

"I'll see what I can do," Shelly had said, laughing.

Then she collected Spike from the comfortable spot he had found on the old Persian rug right outside Nick's inner sanctum, and she left.

She found that her spirits were soaring on the trip to the police station. It wasn't just that she would no longer be threatened by the huge man following her, but that now she was going to find out *why*. It was the inexplicable mystery of the man's several appearances that had really been bothering her. She hated not knowing the underlying reasons for the things that happened around her, but at least in the case of the big man and his dark sedan, that would not continue much longer.

"You stay here, I'll be back," Shelly said to Spike, leaving the car windows down.

Shelly asked for Sergeant Garcia on his floor of the police station and was directed to an interrogation room. She knocked on the heavy soundproof door, which was labeled INTERRO-GATION TWO. A moment later it opened, and Garcia, in uniform but without his hat, ushered her inside. The little room had no windows but did have a large mirror almost as wide as the room. The rest of the walls were covered with acoustic tile. A table filled most of the room, and on the opposite side, facing the mirror, was the huge man.

He looked gigantic even sitting down, but under the bright fluorescent lights he didn't seem so menacing. He looked at Shelly when she entered and then looked quickly away. There was a styrofoam cup half filled with coffee in front of him and a couple of torn and empty sugar packets. He took a sip of the coffee.

"Have a seat, Shelly," Sergeant Garcia said, joining her on the side of the table opposite the large man. "This is Mr. Michael Morrison, who was a client of your father's. Mr. Morrison has some things he wants to say to you."

Mr. Morrison set his styrofoam cup back on the table and flattened his hands around it. Staring at them, Shelly thought his fists would be as big as softballs.

"I didn't mean to scare you," the big man said in a surprisingly soft voice. "I'm afraid I haven't handled this very well. It's just been very upsetting, and I guess I haven't been thinking right recently."

"Why don't you start at the beginning, Mr. Morrison," Sergeant Garcia suggested.

The big man nodded. "Sure. See, I own a few grocery stores—Morrison's. Maybe you've heard of them?"

Shelly nodded. There was one less than a mile from her house.

"I've got seventeen stores all along the coast from Maine to Maryland, and I have to travel a lot to keep an eye on them. I don't like it, but it goes with the territory. My wife, she's a district court judge. For a while there, we weren't getting along too well and I started thinking she was having an affair when I was out of town. So I hired this P.I. to find out—"

"My dad," Shelly guessed.

Mr. Morrison snorted. "I wish. No, a friend of mine—whose credibility is now zero, let me tell you—recommended this guy Artie Hanks."

Shelly remembered her father's mention of the man—"a real slimy character" he had called him.

"So this guy Hanks follows my wife around, and sure enough, she's having an affair. Hanks took pictures and everything, for use in divorce proceedings. Only we didn't get divorced. I showed my wife the pictures, and we yelled and screamed and...well, we worked it out. We've been married twelve years, and a lot of bad feelings had built up, but after we got them out in the open, they disappeared. End of story, I thought."

Mr. Morrison paused for a sip of coffee.

"But not for Hanks. He sees there isn't going to be a divorce. With seventeen grocery stores, he knows I've got money. My wife, she's a judge. If those pictures got sent to, say, the newspapers her career would be ruined. My wife made a mistake, but she's a good woman, and a good judge. She doesn't deserve that. Hanks wanted me to pay him to make sure it didn't happen."

Morrison shook his head. "The amount he wanted wasn't so bad. I could have afforded it, but it made me mad. So I did more research this time around and I hired me a private eye I could trust."

"My father," Shelly said softly.

He nodded. "I found out there was no love lost between him and Hanks, so I went to him and laid it all out for him. Made him almost as mad as it made me. And while I was doing this, the stakes got raised. My wife found out she was being considered for a seat on the Massachusetts State Supreme Court. It wasn't in the news yet, but it would be in a few days. If Hanks found that out while he still had those negatives, he wouldn't settle for a measly five thousand dollars—he'd squeeze me for everything he could get.

"So your father said he'd handle it. I'm not sure what he did. I think maybe Hanks was a little afraid of him, that if your father really put his mind to it, Hanks would be doing time in a cage somewhere. Anyway, your father talked to him and got him to settle for a couple thousand.

DEAD MAN'S CONFESSION 203

He turned the negatives over to your father and had himself a good laugh. He'd forced the great R. Sherlock Holmes to pay up, and he felt like he'd won. Your father let him think that, let him laugh all he wanted. Two days later my wife was named to the Supreme Court, and it was your dad and me who were laughing. Hanks must have been pulling his hair out when he realized he could have gotten a hundred times as much money."

"That's my dad," Shelly murmured.

"My problem is," Morrison continued, looking down at his hands again, "that I was out of town when your father dealt with Hanks. He told me how it went down over the phone, but I never saw him again. I was supposed to meet him to get the negatives from him Saturday morning, but . . . ."

"He was killed Friday night," Shelly finished for him.

Morrison nodded. "I went to the funeral and was going to talk to you there, but it didn't seem right. So I waited until yesterday and went to try the office, but you ran at the sight of me. I went to your house, figuring that's where you would go, but didn't see you. I finally found out where you were staying by calling your aunt and telling her I needed to discuss a scholarship with you. Your dad had mentioned you were graduating high school. She gave me the phone number, and I had a friend at the phone company get the address for me. When I got there, you were leaving. I guess following you and trying to talk to you in a vacant parking lot was a dumb idea…"

"You got that right, pal," Sergeant Garcia interjected.

"…but I'm desperate to get those negatives back and destroy them. My wife deserves everything she's getting, and I don't want it ruined."

Shelly nodded. "Why the hurry, though? If Dad had them I'm sure they're in the safe in the office. Nobody's going to get at them there."

"Hanks is after them," Morrison said passionately. "He called me late Saturday night to tell me I shouldn't have gone to your father and that once he got the negatives back I was really going to have to pay. You don't know what an . . . an *evil* man he is."

Sergeant Garcia nodded. "That one-armed sleaze is the lowest form of life," he agreed.

Shelly's skin went cold. *"One-armed?"*

Chapter Seventeen

After her strange outburst, Sergeant Garcia and Morrison both looked at her sharply.

"Yeah," Sergeant Garcia said. "The creep's only got one arm."

Shelly told him about the break-in at her father's office, and the one-armed silhouette she had seen that day.

"Sounds like Hanks all right," Sergeant Garcia said. "But you didn't see his face?"

Shelly shook her head. "There wasn't enough light."

"He's probably the one who tore up your parents' house, too," Sergeant Garcia said, "but if you can't identify him, we can't make a case. He'll claim you saw some other one-armed man, and he'll fabricate himself an alibi for the day. That kind of thing is his stock-in-trade."

"When he broke in," Morrison asked anxiously, "do you think he got the negatives?"

"I haven't checked the safe since then," Shelly said, "but I doubt it. He didn't have time with the alarm having been set off. Besides, I think you probably would have heard from him last night if he did. But just to be sure—and to get this taken care of once and for all—why don't we go down to the office now. Sergeant Garcia, would you mind coming along?"

"My pleasure, Miss Holmes," he responded.

They went downstairs and split up at the parking lot. Shelly took the Lincoln with Spike, and Sergeant Garcia brought Morrison along in his police cruiser. They met in the underground parking garage and rode the elevator together up to the lobby. Shelly could hear Spike barking; he didn't like the idea of being left in the car, again.

The security guard on duty was not one Shelly knew, so she had to show him her I.D. card, and Morrison and Sergeant Garcia had to sign in as visitors.

"You're coming in kind of late, aren't you?" the guard joked.

"There's no time for rest on the trail of the truth," Shelly replied automatically. It was something her father always used to say to her mother when she fretted about the long hours he was working.

They went up in the elevator, and Shelly let them into the office, taking care to deactivate the alarm. She turned to Sergeant Garcia and Morrison in the outer office and said, "If you gentlemen would please wait here, I'll only be a minute."

She entered the inner office by herself and closed the doors behind her. Then she went to the low oak cabinet and slid the top out of the way to reveal the safe. Once it was open, she

removed the box of letters and photos from
Grandpa Emmet and searched through the other
files and documents stacked inside. It didn't take
long. Near the top was a manila envelope with
the name Morrison across the top in her father's
strong handwriting. She closed and concealed
the safe once again, and then returned to the
outer office.

"I think this is what everyone's been so interested in," Shelly said, holding up the manila
envelope. She handed it to Morrison, who was
sitting on the sofa. Sergeant Garcia was slowly
pacing the carpet in the center of the office.
While Morrison looked in the envelope, Shelly
went to Mrs. Dunn's desk and found a pack of
matches in the top drawer. Carrying the matches
and the empty metal trash can from beneath the
desk, Shelly walked over to where Mr. Morrison
was sitting.

"Is that them?" Shelly asked.

"Yes," Morrison answered. "The negatives are
in here. This is such a relief. I don't know how
to thank you."

"You can thank me by destroying them here
and now." She set the trash can on the floor and
held the matches out toward Morrison.

Morrison looked surprised and suddenly nervous. "That's all right," he said. "I'll do it when
I get home. I don't want to get your office all
smoky."

"I don't mind," Shelly said.

"It might set off the fire alarm," Morrison pointed out.

"If it does, I'll call the security guard and tell him it was a false alarm." Shelly was still holding out the matches. "It occurs to me that your relationship with your wife might not be as stable as you say, Mr. Morrison. It also occurs to me that with those pictures in your possession, you would clearly have the upper hand in that relationship. Maybe I'm just being cynical, but I would prefer not having to wonder if I made a mistake by giving you those photos."

Sergeant Garcia blinked at Shelly and then narrowed his eyes at Morrison. "Do it," he said.

Morrison reluctantly reached out and took the matches. While Shelly and Sergeant Garcia looked on, he burned the manila envelope. In a minute, there was nothing left but flakes of black ash in the trash can. "Happy?" he said.

Shelly nodded. "Give my regards to your wife."

By the time Shelly and Spike got back to the apartment, she could barely keep her eyes open. Gail was still at work on her computer, and after saying good night to her Shelly went to bed.

The next morning she finally found Julie and Gail together, having breakfast in the kitchen. They greeted her when she walked in.

"Good morning," she said back to them. "There's something I want to talk to you both about."

Gail wedged her spoon in the half of a cantaloupe in front of her and twisted around to face Shelly. Julie folded the newspaper she had been reading and looked up expectantly.

"First I want to thank both of you. You've always made me feel welcome here, and I think of you both as my two older sisters. This past week you've been especially sweet, and I wanted to let you know I appreciate it."

"Oh no, she's leaving," Gail murmured, exchanging a concerned look with Julie.

"You can't go back to that house..." Julie began to say, but Shelly cut her off.

"I don't want to go back to that house," she said. "My parents' will named my aunt and uncle my legal guardians. They wanted me to move in with them, but I told them I would rather live here, with you. They said it was all right with them, so now I'm asking if it's all right with you. I'll pay a share of the rent and food, and do my part of the cooking and cleaning..."

Gail and Julie erupted in laughter. "You don't have to sell us, girl," Gail said.

"Gail and I already talked about this," Julie said. "We had this whole speech put together on why you should stay here, but I guess we didn't need it. Of course you can live here."

"Oh, but I don't know," Gail said, looking suddenly serious. "We neglected to ask our third roommate."

"That's right," Julie said. "Sorry, Shelly but this is a democracy. Spike!"

The German shepherd's face poked in the kitchen doorway a moment later and found them all staring at him. He looked back over his shoulder.

"Come here, Spike," Shelly called, clapping her hands on her thighs.

Spike bounced forward and jumped up, pinning Shelly against the refrigerator with his forepaws. He started licking her face while she laughed helplessly.

"Well, looks like it's unanimous," Gail said, pulling her spoon loose and turning her attention back to the cantaloupe.

"Welcome to the funhouse, Shelly," Julie said as she opened the newspaper again. "You're now an official inmate."

After Gail and Julie left for the university, Shelly propped herself on the living room sofa and started reading the journal of Charles Lapidis, Sr. She quickly realized that, unlike her, Lapidis had not been a faithful chronicler of his life and times. Rarely had he written entries more frequently than two days in a row, and sometimes there were gaps of weeks or more between them.

Shelly started at the beginning and read every word, as she believed the best way to determine where he had hidden the land title was to get to know the man as well as possible, get to know the way his mind worked. The journal entries were dated and started about two years before the date on R. J. Tambler's letter to Shelly's great-grandfather.

In the opening pages Mr. Lapidis revealed that he had begun to keep this diary to express his feelings for a woman with whom he professed to be in love. Her name was Rosalind, and she was the daughter of a banker. Mr. Lapidis had spoken to her frequently at local affairs and had once escorted her to the theater. Shelly didn't think this added up to a deep commitment, but apparently Mr. Lapidis did. Rosalind had turned down several other invitations to see him since, and he spent pages trying to decipher her motives. To Shelly it seemed obvious—she didn't like him—but Mr. Lapidis seemed to think someone, her father perhaps or some other man in her life, was influencing her, keeping her away from him, for Mr. Lapidis was sure Rosalind wanted to be with him. When one day she suddenly announced her impending marriage to a sailor and moved with him to his home in Virginia, Mr. Lapidis finally knew who the culprit was.

Mr. Lapidis tried to find out more about this sailor and perhaps get even with him somehow, but Virginia was outside his sphere of influence. The entries became sparse for a while, and then they picked up with the appearance of R. J. Tambler. Mr. Lapidis referred to him most often as "the sailor." Though he was not the same seaman who had taken his beloved Rosalind away, it was obvious to Shelly that Mr. Lapidis saw him as one of the same breed and someone on whom to take his vengeance for the loss of Rosalind.

The land deal was mentioned. Not long after, Mr. Lapidis outlined his scheme to dupe R. J. Tambler, but he did it in such a circumspect way that it seemed more a fantasy than a plan he had intended to carry out. Sentences such as "If I were a spiteful man, I could convince the sailor to make our bargain in secrecy" were not a bald-faced confession, but Shelly had no doubt that this accurately described what had taken place.

After the deal had been struck and Mr. Tambler had learned how he'd been swindled, Mr. Lapidis's entries became joyful. His words sang with the strength of his satisfaction, and he faithfully recorded each encounter he had with the man and how he rubbed salt in his emotional wounds and baited him mercilessly.

Shelly finally reached an entry in which Mr. Lapidis good-humoredly recorded an encounter with Mr. Tambler in which he teased him by mentioning that the real land title existed. He speculated that "the sailor" might be so crazed at this point that he might actually break into the Lapidis house to search for the title. "I do so hope he does!" Mr. Lapidis wrote. "For I've got my servants on the watch for his sorry face and ordered them to ring the police if he's seen. He can rend the place to pieces for hours and not find the title where I've tucked it safely 'twixt London's leaves, by which time the police will have arrived and I'll see the scoundrel in prison!"

"'London's leaves,'" Shelly said aloud. He buried it beneath a tree from England, perhaps? Or "leaves" could mean the removable sections that let you make a table longer or shorter. Perhaps he had a table made in London, and he concealed the title in that.

Shelly put her speculations on hold and finished reading the journal. There was not much left. R. J. Tambler had not taken Lapidis's bait and had begun to avoid him. Mr. Lapidis himself had other concerns, and about a year after the land swindle he met the woman who would become his wife. That seemed to mark the end of his interest in R. J. Tambler, as well as the end of his interest in keeping a journal.

Shelly closed the journal and stared at the ceiling for a few minutes, trying to figure out how she could check on the trees and tables at

Lapidis's house. English trees—there was an English walnut tree, Shelly knew, but how did you hide something between its leaves? You could bury something at the base of it, but Mr. Lapidis had said, " …'twixt London's leaves." Between the leaves. Shelly began flipping absently through the journal as she switched theories and wondered how to track down an English table from seventy years ago. The pages were flipping through her fingers….

Pages. She sat straight up. *Leaves* was sometimes another word for the pages of a book. Lapidis was an avid book collector.

Shelly ran to collect her car keys. Spike on her heels, she flew down the steps of the apartment.

She burst into Baker Street Books so abruptly that Nick jumped behind the counter, where he had been intent on the computer nestled back there between stacks of books.

"What? Oh, hello, Shelly," he said. "How are you?"

"The game's afoot," Shelly said.

A light went on in Nick's eyes. "How so?" he whispered.

"I know where the genuine land title is hidden!" she announced. She looked around, suddenly embarrassed, but fortunately there were no customers in the store at the moment.

"Where?" Nick asked.

"Wait just a moment. In the books we went through last night, do you remember seeing any by Jack London?"

"Yes, I believe so. Several first editions in fact—*The Call of the Wild, White Fang, The Sea Wolf...*"

"That's it!" Shelly said. "Oh, what a twisted sense of humor Mr. Lapidis had. Come on, Nick, we've got to find that book again."

Nick locked the front door and flipped the sign in the window from OPEN to CLOSED without a moment's hesitation and then followed Shelly into his inner sanctum. They took up the positions they had spent so much time in last night and began going back through the boxes they had unpacked and repacked less than 24 hours ago. While they looked, Shelly explained what she had read in Lapidis's journal, about him having a psychological grudge against sailors because he viewed them all as the man who had taken Rosalind from him.

"So he hid the title in a book about sailors," Nick said. "I have to agree with you. That is surely the act of a man with a twisted sense of humor."

They dug through the boxes for fifteen minutes before Nick put his hands on the right book. "Here it is, Shelly," he said, and then he reverently handed it to her.

She held the book up and riffled the pages, to see if anything would fall out. A doubt struck her: What if the title had fallen out and been lost years ago? She put the book on top of Nick's rolltop desk, in the circle of light provided by the gooseneck lamp, and looked at it more closely. Inside the front cover, it looked normal. Inside the back cover, the end paper had been glued unevenly, and there was a slight, square bulge beneath.

Shelly grinned at Nick. "There it is."

She moved to let Nick take a closer look. "The end paper has definitely been torn free and reglued," he said in a disapproving voice. Nick reacted to people abusing books as others reacted to people abusing children. "Well, doing it one more time isn't going to hurt it."

He searched in the drawers of the desk and turned up a single-edged razor blade. Carefully, he started at the top close to the binding and slit the end paper free of the cover. He did this all the way around three sides so the end paper flapped loose like the pages of the book themselves. Then he lifted the end paper and revealed a rectangle of folded brown paper. He removed it gently and then moved the book aside. Using a pair of forceps so as not to break the brittle paper, he carefully began to unfold it. It had been folded in half, and in half again. He didn't unfold it completely, or it would have broken into four quarters along the fold lines, but he did open it enough so that they could read the writing which referred to property in Barnstable County, Massachusetts. At the bottom, next to the word "Owners" were the clear signatures of Charles Lapidis and R. J. Tambler.

Nick looked up at Shelly, excitement once again filling his eyes. "Amazing, Holmes," he said. "You astound me."

"Elementary," Shelly replied, with a satisfied smile.

Chapter Eighteen

Several days later, Shelly found herself seated in the agency's outer office with a TV camera trained on her. She was wearing the most professional outfit she had, a charcoal skirt/jacket combo with a white blouse. Jackie Tambler occupied the chair facing her and held a microphone in one hand. At the moment, Shelly was speaking into it.

"...and after we found the real land title, it was turned over for verification. Then, well, you know the rest."

The rest, the details of which Shelly and Jackie had mutually decided not to go into on TV, was that the Tambler family received an impressive settlement from the current owners of the land R. J. Tambler had purchased seventy years ago. Today it was occupied by a shopping mall and several corporate office plazas, and the challenge of ownership had been big news. The owners needed to assure the tenants who leased space in their buildings that there was no problem and settled quickly and without much of a fight. In recognition of the part she had played, Shelly had been awarded 15 percent of the final settlement amount.

Jackie shifted the microphone back to herself.

DEAD MAN'S CONFESSION 219

"Can you tell us what the future holds for the Holmes Investigative Agency?"

Shelly said, "We're officially back open as of today. The staff is a remarkably capable group of professionals." Out of the corner of her eye, Shelly could see Mrs. Dunn and John Lane exchange smiles and a few words. "I've gotten a lot of support from both them and my family."

"And what exactly is your role in this?" Jackie asked.

"I'm in charge," Shelly said, and then laughed with Jackie. "I'm not yet a licensed private investigator, so I won't be handling cases directly myself, but I'll be overseeing things."

"So the Holmes Agency will continue with a Holmes overseeing operations," Jackie said.

"That's right."

"And what are your personal plans for the future?"

"I had been planning on attending college this fall at the University of Colorado," Shelly said, "but I can't run the agency from two thousand miles away. Instead, I've applied at Boston College as a criminal justice major. Someone whose opinion I trust a lot recommended Boston College very highly to me." Shelly, having remembered her mother's enthusiastic description, had visited the campus yesterday, had decided on the spot she wanted to go there, and had gotten the materials to apply. With her academic record she didn't think she'd have any problem getting in.

Jackie said, "Well, from your record so far it doesn't look like you'll need it, but I wish you good luck for the future."

"Thanks, Jackie," Shelly said.

Jackie turned to the camera operator and drew her finger across her throat. "That's it, guys. Break it down." As the camera operator and his assistant began to take down the lights they'd erected in the office, Jackie turned back to Shelly. "You were terrific."

"I was terrified," Shelly said. "I didn't seem too nervous?"

"Not at all," Jackie said. "Very professional, in fact."

"Thanks. I don't know how you do this all the time. It must be a lot of pressure."

"And I don't know how you pulled off keeping this agency going, but it looks like you're doing all right. You could probably teach me a thing or two about pressure." Jackie stood, to follow her crew out. She'd already explained they needed to hurry to get the tape edited and ready for tonight's broadcast. "You've still got my card, right? Stay in touch. I'm rooting for you."

"I'll do that," Shelly called as they left. "Thanks again."

After the doors closed behind them, John and Mrs. Dunn started clapping.

"Bravo!" Mrs. Dunn called out.

"Wonderful performance," John added. "Your 'remarkably capable group of professionals' is proud of their boss."

Shelly laughed "And as the boss, I find myself compelled to ask: Shouldn't you be out on that case we got this morning?"

John held up his hands. "Okay, okay. I just wanted to catch your television debut. I'm on it now."

Shelly waved fondly as he slipped out. The truth was they were all in terrific spirits since this morning. The first day officially open with Shelly in charge and they had already gotten a case. John was handling it officially, but Shelly had sat in on the initial consultation. The client, a coin dealer whose store had been robbed and who had heard of Shelly's success on the Tambler case, had insisted on it.

Shelly and Mrs. Dunn returned to what they had been doing before the interview. Mrs. Dunn was teaching her all about the operation of the agency. Shelly wanted to be aware of every detail, even though Mrs. Dunn looked after most of them.

The phone rang soon after. It was a reporter from the *Herald* looking for a quick interview, and Shelly had no sooner gotten off the line with him than someone from the *Chicago Tribune* called. They were calling from all over the country! Shelly had had a meeting with John, Mrs. Dunn, and her Uncle Joe yesterday to discuss her running the agency, and it had been pointed out to her that the press was good, free publicity if she took advantage of it, and she was. She was friendly to each reporter and answered each question as best she could. Her father had had a good relationship with the press, Uncle Joe had said, cooperating with them when he could so when he couldn't talk about a case they usually respected his silence. Shelly was trying to build the same kind of relationship.

So it happened that Shelly ended up at the office late that evening, talking to a reporter on the West Coast. She had sent Mrs. Dunn home at five and had spent the rest of the time between phone calls familiarizing herself with the contents of the safe, so there would be no more surprises like Mr. Morrison's photographs. Finally she decided it was time to quit and head for home.

She took the elevator down to the parking garage and headed for the Lincoln, looking forward to watching herself on the news with Gail, Julie and Spike. Such pleasant thoughts made it even more of a shock when a one-armed shadow stepped out from behind one of the garage's concrete supports.

Shelly stopped and took stock of her surroundings. There were at least a dozen cars still left in the garage, from other people working late, but there was no one else in the garage at the moment. She was maybe ten steps from the one-armed man. It was another twenty beyond him to her car, or fifty back to the elevator. Then she took a second to think. her impulse was to flee, but why should she? She knew what Hanks wanted and that he was out of luck.

"The pictures and negatives have been destroyed," Shelly said, using the same professional voice she'd used during the interview with Jackie.

"So you know about the pictures," Hanks said, ambling closer. He wore a long-sleeved coat, with the one empty sleeve pressed flatly against his side. He scratched his unshaven cheek with his hand. "You're sure they were destroyed?"

"I had Michael Morrison over to the office a few nights ago," Shelly answered. "He took a little convincing from a police friend of mine, but in the end he saw it my way and burned them to ashes. Nothing left. You're just going to have to find someone else to blackmail, Hanks."

"So the little girl knows my name," he mused.

"And your game," Shelly said. "You're an opportunistic vulture and a general discredit to the profession."

"Am I now?" he said. "Your father must have mentioned me. Do you miss him?" He was so close now she could smell his sour breath.

"That's a stupid question," Shelly said heatedly.

"Not me," Hanks said. "Not one bit."

Shelly smiled coldly. "That's because he beat you. Because he was ten times the detective you could ever be. He was at the highest level of the profession, and you—you're the lowest."

Hanks squinted one eye at her. "You've got a big mouth for such a pretty girl."

Shelly expected him to say more. When he didn't, she said, "So?"

He chuckled. "I hear you're taking over the business. You're the new Sherlock on the block. That right?"

Shelly nodded. "That's right."

He put his hand in the pocket of his coat, and for a second Shelly thought he was going to pull out a gun. "In that case, we're probably going to be running into each other again." He spun around and started walking away, his footsteps loud in the echoing garage. "See you around, Holmes."

Shelly watched him for a moment as he headed for the exit. Then she hurried to her car and got inside. She locked the door, just like her father had always told her to. Now she knew why.

When Shelly reached the apartment, she was

disappointed to find no other cars in the driveway. Gail and Julie must be working late at the
university, she thought. She had been looking
forward to watching the news with them, but at
least Spike was home. She supposed she could
tape it for them, but it wouldn't be the same.

At the top of the stairway, Shelly opened the
door with her key and paused. She peered
inside, through the entryway to the living room
and the kitchen doorway. It was completely
dark. Gail and Julie always left the kitchen light
on, so they could find their way around at night
without risking bruised knees and stubbed toes.
Something was wrong.

And where was Spike? Never had he failed to
greet her at the door before. Shelly was thinking
of closing the door without going in and then
going to call the police, but there was a strong
odor in the air coming from inside. She stood in
the doorway, sniffing, trying to identify it. It
was so familiar. And then she had it: It
was...*pepperoni*?

Suddenly all of the lights came on and familiar faces appeared from behind furniture and
doorways. "Surprise!" they chorused. Shelly had
worked herself up to such a state of wariness that
this sudden light and noise nearly made her
jump off the stairway. Then she smiled weakly
with relief and entered the apartment.

Spike came bounding out of Gail's bedroom,

where she had been restraining him, and nearly knocked Shelly over with his enthusiastic welcome. As she returned his greeting, Shelly spotted Julie coming out of the kitchen with Kay and Maria. Amanda slipped out of the front closet. Her older cousins Peggy and Heather had been hiding behind the sofa in the living room, and 12-year-old Russell hopped from behind a row of plants in the front window. Toby, it seemed, had been hiding behind the front door and startled her again when she realized he was there.

"What's going on?" Shelly asked, smiling bewilderedly.

"Hm," Amanda said, glancing around appraisingly. "Let's look at this like a detective. We've got people. We've got pizza. We've got soda. Couldn't be a party, could it, Holmes?"

"Brilliant deduction, Blaine," Shelly said, laughing at her friend. "Can you tell me why?"

Julie answered, "So we can celebrate the reopening of the agency."

"And watch your television debut," Kay added.

"We've got our VCRs all set up," Amanda said. "We can't wait to see what you look like in fast-forward and reverse."

Everyone laughed, and then Gail led them into the kitchen, where several pizzas were laid out next to a huge salad and a colorful array of soda cans. Shelly filled a plate, grabbed a soda, and then went into the living room, where the TV was already on and tuned to the right station. Toby was the next to join her, and for a moment they were alone, with the sounds of good-natured arguing over the last piece of pepperoni coming from the kitchen.

Shelly had sat Indian-style on the floor in front of the TV, and Toby sat next to her. "I haven't had a chance to say so yet, Shelly," he said in a shy way that made Shelly smile, "but I really admired how you figured out where that land title was hidden. Seventy years later, and you made it sound simple."

"Thanks, Toby. That's sweet."

He nodded and returned her smile. "You're going to do great running the agency. Everybody thinks so. I was just wondering," he said, and now he seemed unsure of himself, "do you think you're going to have time for us to, you know, to see each other?"

She reached out to his chin and gently turned his head so she was looking in his eyes. "If there isn't, I'll make time. I've liked you since I first met you, even though I didn't know you very well. Now that I know you better, I like you even more."

Toby took her hand from his chin and held it in his own. "I feel the same way." He paused for a second and then laughed. "I feel like I should give you a ring or something. Does this mean we're officially boyfriend and girlfriend?"

Shelly leaned over and gave him a quick kiss. "Now we are."

Spike barked.

Amanda came out of the kitchen at that moment and exclaimed, "We can't leave you two alone for a second!"

"What's your point?" Shelly asked, slightly embarrassed and focusing her attention on the food on her plate.

The arrival of Shelly's cousins and Julie saved her from further needling. The conversation turned to the agency as the others asked questions about her plans. She was tempted to tell them of her run-in with Artie Hanks and how she had stood toe-to-toe with him without backing down, but the person she really wanted to tell, the one who would really understand and whose respect meant the most to her, was her father. She could picture the expression on his face as she told him the details, the way his eyes would narrow as he pictured the events in his mind. And when she was finished, he would be wearing that proud, loving smile he smiled just for her. Her special smile.

She had to blink several times to keep from crying, and Julie looked at her with wary concern, but Shelly just smiled at her and waved.

By the time the pizzas had been whittled down to a few lonely slices and a pyramid of empty soda cans had been erected on the coffee table, it was time for the news. Everyone watched raptly when Shelly's segment came on. Except for a chorus of excited squeals when her face first appeared on the screen, no one spoke during the interview.

It had been edited to cut out Shelly's few hesitations and made her responses to Jackie's questions seem quick and crisp, altogether professional. Shelly was very pleased with herself, and after the interview, when everyone in the room applauded so loudly that Spike started barking, she stood up and took a bow.

Julie joined her in standing and raised her soda can. "I propose a toast," she said. "To Shelly Holmes, and the successful conclusion of her very first case, the first of many in what I do not doubt will prove to be a long, illustrious, and very exciting career."

The others raised their drinks and chorused their agreement and approval. Shelly joined them in drinking, Julie's words still echoing in her head. Her first case. The first of many.

She liked the sound of that.

DON'T MISS

Adventures of Shelly Holmes™ Case #2

Till Death Do Us Part

COMING SOON!

A missing bridegroom, missing money, and a missing boyfriend are the ingredients in yet another suspense-filled, exciting Shelly Holmes mystery adventure.

You're invited as Shelly Holmes walks down the aisle with danger.

About the Author

Cass Lewis lives in Bergen County, New Jersey, with her husband Ron and their dog Spike. She is a fan of both Nancy Drew and Sherlock Holmes and therefore thoroughly enjoys writing the Adventures of Shelly Holmes.

Cass hopes her readers will join her for the next exciting adventure of Shelly Holmes.